Readers love *At Your Service*
by ARIEL TACHNA

"*At Your Service* is a beautifully written tale where two guys rise from the despair of heartbreak to find and experience the true meaning of love."
—QUEERcentric Books

"If you're looking for a nice read with two endearing characters—and also Paris—then definitely pick this one up."
—Joyfully Jay

"This is a lovely, sexy, emotional, hopeful story. Love can win the day if you are willing to fight for it!"
—*Divine Magazine*

"If you love your stories with some angst, travel and struggles towards romance, then *At Your Service* by Ariel Tachna is the story for you. I absolutely recommend it."
—Scattered Thoughts and Rogue Words

I0659688

More praise for
ARIEL TACHNA

Château d'Eternité

"…this is a very romantic, passionate story… Thanks, Ariel, for the stimulating visit to the past."

—Rainbow Book Reviews

"I found this to be a very engaging story of self-discovery and love."

—Live Your Life, Buy the Book

Testament to Love

"I can count on Ariel to give me a fantastic story; she does wonderful things with big intense novels, and sweet little ones like this."

—Love Bytes

The Path

"…never have I felt so connected, so involved in the past and present as I did here in The Path… I read this book twice, and each time its magic grew as did its hold on my imagination and heart."

—Scattered Thoughts and Rogue Words

"This story is one of growth, of passion, and of two men who are so right for each other that words cannot do it justice. The Path is just a really excellent read."

—Joyfully Jay

By ARIEL TACHNA

Best Ideas
Château d'Eternité
With Nessa L. Warin: Dance Off
Fallout
Her Two Dads
Highland Lover
Home for Chirappu
In Search of Fireworks
The Inventor's Companion
The Matelot
Music of the Heart
Once in a Lifetime
Out of the Fire
Overdrive
The Path
Popcorn Garlands
Rediscovery
Revelations in the Dark
Rose Among the Ruins
Seducing C.C.
Stolen Moments
A Summer Place
With Madeleine Urban: Sutcliffe Cove
Testament to Love
Why Nileas Loved the Sea

Published by DREAMSPINNER PRESS
www.dreamspinnerpress.com

By ARIEL TACHNA (CONT.)

AT YOUR SERVICE
At Your Service • Service with a Smirk

DREAMSPUN DESIRES
LEXINGTON LOVERS
#8 – Unstable Stud
#19 – A Matchless Man

GAMES LOVERS PLAY
Amorous Liaison • Best Behavior • Ride 'em Cowboy

HOT CARGO
Healing in His Wings
With Nicki Bennett: Hot Cargo • Something About Harry

LANG DOWNS
Inherit the Sky • Chase the Stars • Outlast the Night
Conquer the Flames • Cherish the Land

PARTNERSHIP IN BLOOD
Alliance in Blood • Covenant in Blood • Conflict in Blood
Reparation in Blood • Perilous Partnership • Reluctant Partnerships
Lycan Partnership • Partnership Reborn • Partnership Reforged

With Nicki Bennett
Under the Skin

ALL FOR LOVE
Checkmate • All for One • Stronghold

THE EXPLORING LIMITS SERIES
Exploring Limits • Stretching Limits • Refining Limits
Breaking Limits • Transcending Limits • No Limits

Published by DREAMSPINNER PRESS
www.dreamspinnerpress.com

ARIEL TACHNA

SERVICE
WITH A
Smirk

DREAMSPINNER
PRESS

Published by
DREAMSPINNER PRESS

5032 Capital Circle SW, Suite 2, PMB# 279, Tallahassee, FL 32305-7886 USA
www.dreamspinnerpress.com

This is a work of fiction. Names, characters, places, and incidents either are the product of author imagination or are used fictitiously, and any resemblance to actual persons, living or dead,
business establishments, events, or locales is entirely coincidental.

Service with a Smirk
© 2017 Ariel Tachna.

Cover Art
© 2017 L.C. Chase.
http://www.lcchase.com
Cover content is for illustrative purposes only and any person depicted on the cover is a model.

All rights reserved. This book is licensed to the original purchaser only. Duplication or
distribution via any means is illegal and a violation of international copyright law, subject
to criminal prosecution and upon conviction, fines, and/or imprisonment. Any eBook format
cannot be legally loaned or given to others. No part of this book may be reproduced or
transmitted in any form or by any means, electronic or mechanical, including photocopying,
recording, or by any information storage and retrieval system, without the written permission
of the Publisher, except where permitted by law. To request permission and all other inquiries,
contact Dreamspinner Press, 5032 Capital Circle SW, Suite 2, PMB# 279, Tallahassee, FL
32305-7886, USA, or www.dreamspinnerpress.com.

ISBN: 978-1-63533-217-9
Digital ISBN: 978-1-63533-218-6
Library of Congress Control Number: 2016915173
Published January 2017
v. 1.0

Printed in the United States of America
(∞)
This paper meets the requirements of
ANSI/NISO Z39.48-1992 (Permanence of Paper).

To Anne, Elizabeth, and Connie, who never stopped believing
I'd finish this, and to Janelle, for giving me permission
to put it on hold until I was actually ready to write it.

CHAPTER 1

PASCAL LAROCQUE sighed as he tossed his gym bag full of sweaty clothes into the tiny laundry room in his apartment (one of the reasons he was willing to pay the exorbitant rent on this particular unit) and debated his options for the evening.

It had been a little over three weeks since his "ladies" had last come into la Colombe d'Or, the upscale restaurant in downtown Montréal where Pascal spent six days a week as one of three senior waiters, and he hadn't even opened the latest installment in the Pascal St-Laurent, International Man of Mystery series they'd given him on their last visit to the restaurant in June. He needed to get most of the way through it before they came back for their monthly dinner, or he'd never hear the end of it. A quiet evening at home held a certain appeal after the busy week he'd had, but Benjamin and René had cornered him at the gym, insisting he come out with them for drinks at Le Salon rather than spend a rare Saturday night off at home.

Grumbling under his breath at the inconvenience of having pushy friends, he went into the bathroom to clean up so he could go out.

An hour later he sat at a corner table, sipping his martini and waiting for his friends. If they didn't show, he was never going out with them again.

The eye candy at Le Salon was always worth the trip, but as Pascal looked around, he saw several new faces among the bartenders and servers bringing drinks to the patrons.

One of these days he'd have to stop looking at them the way he did. He was getting close to an age where he was old enough to be their father. He liked to think he didn't look it, except for the hint of gray at his temples. He certainly didn't feel it, but that didn't change the numbers. He was forty-eight, and he'd bet not one of the guys he was currently staring at was over twenty-five. Adrien, the lounge owner, wouldn't hire them unless they were twenty—he gave them two years after they were of legal age to get a little maturity before he hired them—but he knew his crowd. The young ones drew more patrons than the ones over thirty.

"You need a refill on that?" The server was one of the new ones, a cute twink sporting short spiky brown hair with bleached-blond tips, a flirty smile, and the tightest T-shirt known to man.

"Sure," Pascal said. He drained what was left in his glass so he could send the empty away. "I started a tab."

"Adrien told me," the server said, leaning in to get the glass and wipe the table. "He said to take good care of you."

Pascal frowned. Adrien might have said any number of things, but Pascal knew better than to think that was one of them. Either the kid was aiming for a higher tip (bending over provocatively so Pascal could ogle his ass was one thing. Blatantly lying was another), or he was tricking. Pascal wasn't above ogling a tight ass in even tighter jeans, but he came to Le Salon specifically because Adrien's servers weren't hustling on the side.

"What's that look for?" René asked as he joined Pascal at the table. "You don't usually frown at having an ass in your face."

"New server," Pascal said. "He's still a little… rough around the edges."

"And you're still as picky as ever," René deduced.

"Just because it's a bar on rue Sainte-Catherine instead of a restaurant downtown is no excuse for bad service," Pascal insisted.

The young man came back with Pascal's drink, setting it on the table with a flirtatious smile before turning to René. "What can I get for you?"

Pascal frowned again. That tone of voice, the one that seemed to offer more than just drinks, grated on Pascal's nerves.

René had to go and make it worse. Typical, really. "What's… new on the menu?"

The kid leaned in closer, close enough his hip nearly bumped René's shoulder. "I'm sure I could come up with something to surprise you. What do you like? Sweet, sour, dry, bitter?"

"Spicy," René said. "Something with a kick."

Pascal had to look away as René leered at the kid openly. The rate things were going, René would soon be groping him right there at the table. God, he was glad those days were behind him. Twenty years ago he'd done what he needed to do to get enough experience to land a job at a place like la Colombe d'Or. He wouldn't go back for all the tea in China!

"I know just the thing," the server said, and his hip did bump René's shoulder this time. "A chipotle margarita. If you don't like it, it's on me."

Pascal had to give the kid credit for thinking on his feet. That wasn't a drink Pascal would have come up with to suggest, but few of his guests asked for help with cocktails. Wine, all the time, but not cocktails.

He glanced down at the vodka martini, the same thing he always ordered anywhere he went unless he ordered wine, and wondered when he'd ended up in such a rut.

"If this is what I like, what would you suggest for me?" he asked before the kid could leave the table.

"Drinking hard tonight?" René asked.

"Just curious," Pascal retorted, keeping his eyes on the server, not on his friend.

"It depends," the server said. "Are you feeling adventurous, or do you want to play it safe?"

Pascal considered himself a play-it-safe kind of guy, but he read the challenge in the kid's smile. "I could be adventurous."

He kicked René under the table when his friend muttered, "And pigs will fly."

"Well," the server said, "you could go with a flavored martini—pear, pomegranate, raspberry, something like that. Or there's always a cosmo. They'd be similar to what you're already drinking, but with a little something extra. If you're really feeling adventurous, you could go with an Adios Motherfucker."

Pascal quirked an eyebrow at that. "Sounds… intriguing, but I think I'll stick with this for now. Maybe when I finish it, I'll think about your suggestions."

The server shrugged and nodded before leaving the table.

"When pigs fly," René repeated.

"Fuck off," Pascal said with no real heat in his voice. "There's nothing wrong with having a favorite drink."

"Nothing wrong at all," René agreed, "but there's also nothing wrong with trying something new from time to time. You're stuck in a rut, and that's not healthy."

"Are we still talking about my choice of drinks, or was there something else you wanted to say?"

"We're not talking about anything," René said, "because you're old before you're even fifty, set in your ways and not even open to the possibility that life might have something good in store for you still. It's been fifteen years since Robert died. He wouldn't want you to grieve forever."

"It's not about Robert," Pascal insisted. "I'm comfortable with my life the way it is."

"Yes, I'm sure you are," René said, "but you aren't happy."

"And you think screwing around with some twink in a bar restroom will make me happy?" Pascal asked. "How many friends have we lost to exactly that mistake?"

"That was a different time and a different mindset," René reminded him. "We're all a little smarter now."

"Or a lot more cautious," Pascal replied. "Look, I know you mean well, but that isn't what I want. Just… just let me go to hell in my own way, okay?"

René looked like he was about to argue, but whatever he might have said was forestalled by Benjamin's arrival. "Bonsoir, les gars."

"Bonsoir," René and Pascal replied, switching to French now that Benjamin had joined them. While all three of them were bilingual, Benjamin's English was much weaker than his French, so Pascal and René both automatically spoke French when Benjamin was with them.

"Anything interesting happening tonight?" Benjamin asked as he took a seat at their table.

"Adrien has a new waiter," René said. "Cute, blondish, all tousled. Looks like he'd bend over for the first guy to show a little interest."

"Are you interested?" Benjamin asked, waggling his eyebrows teasingly at René. Pascal had long since given up trying to understand their relationship.

"No, Pascal saw him first."

"Oh, Pascal's interested? Now there's a nice switch!"

"I'm not interested," Pascal said with a long-suffering sigh. "I told René that. He's not listening, as usual."

"Maybe if you said something new, I'd be more inclined to pay attention," René retorted. "As it is, it's the same old martyr Pascal as always." He fixed Pascal with a piercing stare. "It's getting old, buddy. Really old."

Pascal frowned. He'd come out despite wanting to stay home purely because his friends had asked him to, and now they were insulting him. He pulled enough cash from his wallet to cover his bill and tossed it on the table. "If you're going to be like that, I'll go home and read the book that's waiting for me. It'll be better company."

"Pascal, don't be like that," Benjamin cajoled. "You know René doesn't mean anything by it."

Pascal looked back and forth between his two friends. Benjamin's expression was pleading, but René's had taken on the mulish look it got when he had a bug up his ass. "I'm sure he doesn't, but I'm not fit company tonight. Maybe later this week."

"You'll be at work the rest of the week," René muttered.

"Then I'll see you at the gym," Pascal replied. It would be easy to sit back down, but if he did that, René would take it as tacit approval to continue their previous line of conversation, something Pascal was determined to avoid.

Benjamin started to say something else, but René shook his head. "Let him go. If he wants to be like that, we can't stop him."

Pascal almost gave in at that. These were his best friends, the men who had supported him through Robert's illness and death, who had stood with him at a rainy cemetery as he had said his last good-byes to the man he'd thought he would spend his life with. He hated to have discord between them, but he wasn't ready for what René was suggesting. He didn't know if he'd ever be ready for it, and hearing his friend harp on it only made it worse.

"I'm sorry," he said before turning toward the door.

He passed the server on his way out. "Leaving already? It's early, and I still haven't convinced you to try a new drink!"

"Another time," Pascal said. "I'm not in the mood for company tonight."

"Too bad. I'll have to wait for another time to draw you out."

That was almost enough to make Pascal consider changing bars, but even he had limits on how much he would let his past control his present. "I'll look forward to it."

Not wanting any more conversation, he brushed past the waiter and headed home.

TWO HOURS later Pascal closed the book with a grin on his face. Martine had outdone herself this time. He had grinned and gasped through the first hundred and fifty pages of the book, and if it weren't well after midnight, he'd keep going. He couldn't stop himself from flipping it back open to the dedication page.

P,
These books wouldn't exist without you and all our
wonderful dinners.
M

It might be Martine's name on the cover of the books, but he'd listened to them discussing books over dinner more than once. They all contributed ideas, regardless of whose book it ended up being. It had taken time for him to get used to the idea that his ladies who came in once a month and always asked to sit as his table were authors. It had taken even more time to get used to the idea that they wrote gay romance, but all of that had been easy compared to the shock of realizing Martine had modeled the hero of a series after him. He was no James Bond, however much fun she had writing stories that cast him as an international superspy and playboy, but he'd very quickly realized she drew more from his suave appearance in the restaurant than anything else. Sure, he shared a first name and some physical characteristics with Pascal St-Laurent, but the resemblance ended there. He considered his ladies friends now, not just customers in the restaurant, but they never included anything personal about him in their books, the Pascal St-Laurent ones or any others they wrote. The character's history or current lifestyle didn't have anything in common with Pascal's own.

Once he'd realized that, he'd embraced the idea of them and their stories with élan, rooting for the fictional Pascal to find the bad guy, thwart the plot, rescue the guy (or occasionally the girl) in distress, sweep said guy or girl off their feet, and then make his way home to the man he really wanted but couldn't have. He'd asked Martine once if Pascal would ever get his happy ending. She hadn't answered, exactly, but the other three promised she'd never leave a hero alone permanently.

Pascal thought that happy ending might be getting a little closer. Jack had finally divorced his shrew of a wife at the beginning of the current book, taking away the biggest impediment to a relationship with the fictional Pascal. Of course that didn't make Jack gay or interested, but Pascal held to the promise Hélène, Camille, and Nicole had made and chose to believe it was the first step. He could wait for it to come to fruition as long as he knew it would happen eventually. At least one of them would be happy.

He glanced at the clock again and opened the book back to where he'd left off reading. The bad guy had just kidnapped his namesake's flirtation and was threatening to do cruel and unspeakable things to him if Pascal didn't give himself up. It was a new twist, one Martine hadn't used before, and Pascal didn't know how the hero would react. The mission always came first, but he usually did his best to minimize collateral damage, and if the bad guy wasn't thwarted now, the collateral damage would be rather significant.

He'd go to the gym between the lunch and dinner shifts instead of going in the morning.

"SO WHO'D you bang in the book this time?" Benjamin asked as he spotted Pascal doing free weights at the gym four days later. "That is the book you were talking about the other night, isn't it?"

"Yes," Pascal said when he finished his set. "And how many times do I have to tell you it isn't me? He looks a little like me, and he has the same name, but that's where the similarity ends."

"Okay, fine," Benjamin said. "Who did *he* bang in the book this time? Girl or guy?"

"Guy," Pascal said. "I told you before Martine only puts a girl in every three or four books, just enough to make it clear he can swing both ways, even if he prefers guys."

"A good setup? Shower sex or maybe on the beach?" Benjamin asked as he and Pascal switched places on the bench.

"You could just buy the book and read it yourself," Pascal said. "I could even get Martine to sign it for you."

"Just answer the question," Benjamin grunted between reps.

"Fine," Pascal muttered. "It was in the sauna at the hotel where the bad guy was supposed to be staying."

"Did this one survive the encounter?"

"Yes, and they parted amicably enough. Pascal never makes any promises."

"Oh, are you talking about the new book?" René asked, joining them. "Are you any closer to getting the guy of your dreams?"

Pascal sighed. "I told you, it isn't me."

"Yeah, yeah," René said. "So are you?"

"Maybe a little," Pascal said. "Jack finally divorced Charlotte, so that's out of the way, at least. Now Pascal can think about approaching him instead of having to stay silent about it all the time. He hasn't said anything to Jack yet, but the ink is barely dry on the divorce papers. It'll probably be another two or three books before enough time has passed for him to say anything."

"She really enjoys torturing you," René said. "How many books have you been waiting for this guy?"

"This is the eighth book in the series," Pascal said, "and the character has been interested in Jack for that long or longer, but if you consider the duration of each book and the length of time that passes between them in the fictional world, it hasn't been all that long. And she isn't torturing me at all. I love the books. The only torture is waiting for the next one to come out."

"They come out pretty quickly, don't they?" Benjamin asked.

"About every six months," Pascal said. "This isn't all she writes, after all. She has to have time for her other projects too."

"Does she bring you copies of the others?" René asked.

"Why? Do you want to borrow those too?" Pascal joked. His friends would read the *Pascal St-Laurent* books because while they had an undercurrent of romance and at least one steamy sex scene per book, they were more suspense/spy stories than romances. Martine's other books were fairly traditional romances, something Pascal's two friends would never admit to wanting to read. Pascal owned every single one of them. He let Martine give him the *Pascal St-Laurent* books, but he insisted on buying the others she'd written as well as all the ones the other three wrote. As generous as his ladies were with their tips, he could support them in their livelihood as well.

"Just curious," René asked. "I have to know what I can tease you about."

"She only gives me copies of the *Pascal St-Laurent* books." The others stayed on the bookshelf in his bedroom, safely away from René's and Benjamin's prying eyes for precisely that reason.

"Did you bring the new one so we could borrow it?" Benjamin asked.

"No," Pascal said. "Not after you practically tore the cover off the last one. If you want to read it, buy your own. They're available at Drawn & Quarterly, or you can get them online as e-books. You don't need to borrow—and ruin—mine."

"But it's so much more fun to borrow yours," René said, "and to read all the things she writes when she signs them for you."

Pascal rolled his eyes. Martine's sense of fun was as big as her smile, and she took great pleasure in signing his books with outlandish dedications. He always laughed when he read them and kissed her cheek in thanks for the joy she and her friends brought with them every time they came into the restaurant. "Those are meant to be private."

"Then you shouldn't have told us about them," René retorted.

"I won't be telling you about any more of them, that's for sure," Pascal said. He glanced over at the clock on the gym wall. "I have to get cleaned up. I have to be back at the restaurant in half an hour."

René and Benjamin jeered at him, but Pascal brushed it off with the ease of many years of friendship. They might drive him crazy and not take as good care of his books as he would like, but they were his best friends, and they'd be there for him no matter what.

It was a reassuring thought.

He hurried into the gym locker room to shower and dress. He'd seen Hélène's name on the reservations list for tonight. He didn't want to keep his ladies waiting.

CHAPTER 2

MATHIAS PERRAS rushed out the door of his apartment on Monday morning. He hated Mondays with a blinding passion that nearly rivaled his love of the Canadiens. As if that weren't enough, he was running late. Six weeks in his new job, and he was already going to be late.

He didn't have any appointments on his calendar until later in the day, but he was still supposed to be at his desk in case someone walked in wanting to talk to one of the bank accounting specialists. He'd never actually had anyone waiting at the door when the bank opened, but with his luck, today would be the day, and he wouldn't be there to help them.

Maybe he'd get lucky and wouldn't have to wait for the métro. If he caught the train right away, he might still make it to work on time.

He hit the door to the street as an older man opened it. Mathias pushed past him with a mumbled, "Excuse me," practically running at that point, but even his haste wasn't enough to stop his brain's automatic cataloguing of the man's appearance: late forties, graying at the temples, fit, which made sense since he was wearing shorts and a sweaty T-shirt. Mathias was halfway down the street before he realized he knew the guy. It was the man he'd flirted with at Le Salon a week ago, the one who'd left without trying an "adventurous" drink. Mathias groaned. He'd been hoping for another chance with the guy, the next time he came into the bar. Adrien said he was a regular. He didn't have time to worry about it now. The job at the bar was a way to pad his budget a little, but he had to focus on the bank. That was where his future lay.

It was too bad, though, because the guy was everything that pushed Mathias's buttons. He'd always had a thing for older guys, the ones with a bit of gray in their hair and more than enough experience under their belts to teach Mathias a thing or two. His friends at university had teased him about looking for a sugar daddy, but that wasn't it at all. Mathias didn't need someone to support him. He just wanted someone with enough experience to have patience with Mathias's youth and occasional misstep. He'd tried dating guys his own age, but it always ended in disaster with one of them flying off the handle and the relationship ending over something Mathias knew, in retrospect, shouldn't have ended anything. Two somewhat serious relationships he'd had with older men had ended, but not like that, not in a temper and an explosion that could have been avoided if one of them had kept their head. He refused to think about the third one. He consoled himself with the fact that he truly hadn't known Daniel was married and that as soon as he'd figured it out, he'd left him. In a jealous rage, but he'd left rather than believing the promises Daniel had made about leaving his wife for Mathias.

His luck held with the métro, a good thing since it had betrayed him with the guy from the bar. The train arrived just as Mathias reached the platform. He couldn't find a seat, not at the height of rush hour, but at least he was in the car, on the way downtown. He could deal with standing up for the fifteen minutes it would take him to get from Papineau to Lucien L'Allier.

He hurried down the street to the bank and slipped in through the employee door two minutes early. He took a deep breath to steady himself as he walked to his office with a casual (he hoped) wave to Louis, one of the other account specialists he'd gotten friendly with since starting his job. Louis smiled and waved back. They'd have time to talk at lunch. For now, they needed to concentrate on their jobs.

The morning passed more quickly than Mathias would have predicted. He ended up opening several new accounts and helping one older lady adjust her retirement savings plan. All in all, he clocked out for his lunch break feeling quite accomplished.

"Hi, Mathias," Louis said when Mathias walked into the break room the bank employees used for lunch.

"Hi, Louis. What are you reading?"

"The new *Pascal St-Laurent* book. Have you read it yet?"

Mathias shook his head as he opened up his lunch bag. He really ought to make more of an effort for lunch than a ham-and-cheese sandwich and a rather sad-looking apple, but that was about as far as his budget would stretch at the moment. "Not yet. Between working here all day and at the bar most evenings, I barely have time to keep up with all the stuff I'm supposed to be reading as part of this training program."

"Have you read any of them?" Louis asked.

"The first four," Mathias said. "I enjoyed them. I just haven't had time for pleasure reading in a long time."

"You really should get caught up," Louis said. "Things are getting interesting between Pascal and Jack."

"The archives manager?" Mathias asked. "I thought he was straight and married."

Louis grinned. "No fishing for spoilers. If you want to know what happens, read the books."

"Someday," Mathias said with a sigh. "I will have free time again someday, right?"

"Yes," Louis replied. "The first six months are the worst as far as getting your feet under you here with the internship program. Once that's past, you'll have gone through all the training stages, and all you'll have left will be the practical parts. That's still work, but it's a lot less stress outside of business hours."

Four and a half more months. Mathias could do four and a half more months. He just had to remind himself this was what he wanted and the hard work and long hours now would pay off in a few years, when he was in a management position and moving up the corporate ladder.

"I think that's the hardest part," Mathias said. "I don't have a lot of free time outside of work as it is, and it feels like every minute I do have is spent poring over the training manuals."

"I warned you about getting a second job," Louis said. "The internship program is hard enough without it."

"I know," Mathias said, "but I have to be able to afford my rent and food, and my salary here doesn't cover my expenses."

Louis pursed his lips like he was biting back a comment, but Mathias already knew what he wasn't saying. Louis thought he should have gotten an apartment in a less expensive neighborhood or found a roommate or done something else to decrease his expenses rather than taking on an extra job to increase his salary. But Mathias had spent too long dreaming of an apartment and a life in the Village, Montréal's gay district, to settle for anything less now.

"So how's the job at the bar going?" Louis asked after a minute. "Are you enjoying it?"

"Enjoying might be too strong a word," Mathias said, "but it's going well. I'm getting to know some of the regulars, and they all tip pretty well."

"With the right incentive?" Louis teased.

"I'm not doing anything but flirting a little," Mathias protested. "There's no harm in that!"

"As long as they don't decide to try to take it a step further."

"I'm perfectly capable of saying no," Mathias said, "and it isn't that kind of place. The owner was very clear about that when I signed the contract. No funny business at the bar, no matter how consensual or who you were involved with, and if a customer won't take no for an answer, come find him or one of the bouncers."

"That's good," Louis said. "I guess you haven't really had time to meet anyone outside of all the work you're doing. If you don't have time to read a book, you don't have time for a boyfriend."

"Well," Mathias said, "it's probably nothing, but I ran into a guy from the bar as I was leaving home this morning. He was coming in from the gym, so he must live in one of the other apartments. Not that that really counts as meeting someone, but, well…."

"You'd like to meet him," Louis finished for him.

"Yeah. He's exactly my type, for whatever that might be worth."

"Being attracted to your partner is always a plus," Louis joked. "Do you know anything else about him?"

"I don't even know his name," Mathias said. "He was at Le Salon on Saturday a week ago. That's the first time I've seen him, but Adrien said he was a regular. I haven't seen him back since then, though."

"Maybe he has an off-shift job," Louis said. "If you saw him coming in from the gym this morning as you were leaving, he didn't have to be at work at nine."

"True," Mathias said. "I hadn't thought of that. But Saturday isn't his regular night off because he wasn't there this weekend."

Louis laughed. "I thought we just said you didn't have time for a boyfriend."

"For this guy, I'd make time," Mathias admitted. "If he's interested, that is."

"Why wouldn't he be?" Louis asked. "Unless he's already with someone, of course."

"Two other men joined him, but while they were pretty obviously friends, they weren't together, I don't think," Mathias said. "I suppose he could have come out without his partner if he has one, but I didn't get that vibe from him. I guess I'll see how things go the next time he comes in and decide what to do from there."

"Don't be too disappointed if you don't see him right away. If he works odd shifts or odd hours, he might not have the same night off every week or even a night off every week. You don't always work the same nights at the bar."

"True," Mathias said. "I guess I'll just have to be patient, or else hope to run into him in the halls again when I'm not late for work."

"Speaking of late for work," Louis said, "I should get back, and you should finish your lunch so you can do the same."

MATHIAS FLOPPED down on his bed, wondering where he was supposed to find the energy to change clothes and walk down the street to Le Salon. It hadn't been a bad day, much better than Monday had been. In fact, it had really been a quite good one. He'd had several interesting meetings with clients, and he'd left the bank feeling like he'd actually done the job he was hired to do instead of just being a trainee. The problem wasn't *what* he'd done, but the fact that he'd had to be "on" all day long, which was draining, and now he had to put on his other "on" face and go to the bar for a five-hour shift. And to top it off, it was Tuesday, usually a slow night at the bar, which meant he wouldn't even get a good haul in tips to make it worth his while.

He shouldn't complain. He'd gotten to work both Friday and Saturday last week, and he was on both nights again this week, so those nights made up for the slower ones. He was just *tired*.

With a heavy sigh, he levered himself off the bed and into the shower. He'd need another one when he got home given he still managed to spill a drink on himself at least once a night, but if he didn't take one now, he wouldn't be awake enough to go in the first place.

When he got out of the shower, he fixed his hair into the spiky style he preferred for the bar, making a complete break with the clean-cut persona he wore to work, and pulled on a tight T-shirt and jeans. One of the other guys at the bar had assured him the way to get the best tips was to look like every man's wet dream, even if all they could do was look.

He pulled on the combat boots he found most comfortable for the hours on his feet, took a deep breath, and headed out.

The bar was quiet when he got there, only a couple of the other servers already working the tables. Mathias left his coat in the small room in the back the waiters used when they had a break and clocked in. He made a round of the tables, making sure none needed to be wiped down, checking saltshakers and the like, generally trying to make himself useful. Adrien hadn't said it outright, but Mathias had noticed the servers who showed initiative seemed to get the better shifts, and Mathias figured he needed all the help he could get in that respect.

He'd been there for about half an hour when he looked up at the sound of the door opening and saw his mystery man from the previous morning. He smiled to himself, feeling all the energy he'd been faking come surging up for real.

"Welcome back," Mathias said when Mystery Man took a seat. "Are you sticking with a martini tonight, or can I talk you into something more adventurous?"

Mystery Man smiled. "You've got a good memory. That's a bonus in this business."

"That sounds like experience talking," Mathias said, hoping to keep the conversation going while things were quiet. He didn't really expect a huge rush on a Tuesday evening, but he'd take what he could get now, just in case.

Mystery Man just laughed, a very nice, deep laugh, not too throaty or fake.

"You didn't answer my question," Mathias prompted when the laughter didn't lead to a reply.

"Yes, it's experience talking." Mystery Man really had the nicest eyes, Mathias noticed. Blue-gray and dancing with merriment.

"What about the other question?" Mathias asked. "What am I bringing you to drink?"

Mystery Man contemplated that for a moment before his smile widened. "Surprise me."

Mathias took that as a compliment. As hesitant as Mystery Man had been the last time he came in, Mathias decided not to go with anything too wild and crazy for a first try. Michel at the bar had been talking about a new drink he wanted to put on the menu with pear and elderflower. That ought to be something different enough to catch Mystery Man's attention while not so over the top that Mathias would lose his interest because of it.

"*Hé*, Michel," he called when he neared the bar. "I need one of your new drinks. I've got a customer wanting something new."

Michel looked up from mixing the drink in his hands and glanced at the patrons in the bar. "Pascal is the only one who doesn't have a drink. He always gets a vodka martini, neat."

Mathias filed the name away for later. "He told me to surprise him this time. I thought your pear martini would be a little something extra without sending him running away screaming."

Michel looked so surprised that Mathias wondered what he'd done wrong. "I don't know how you got him to even think about anything other than his usual, but I'll make the drink for you. Don't blame me if he doesn't like it."

Mathias promised. Michel finished the drink he was working on and put together Mathias's order. Mathias took it back to Pascal with no little trepidation. Sure, the man's friends had teased him about being a stick-in-the-mud the last time they were in together, but Mathias hadn't thought anything of it. Not really. Now, though, he wondered what he'd done to draw the other man out. Pascal hadn't seemed at all impressed with Mathias's usual shtick. He'd left a decent tip, but nothing extravagant, nothing to suggest Mathias had been at all memorable.

"Here you go," Mathias said, setting the drink down in front of Pascal. "One surprise special."

"Is that what it's called?" Pascal's voice betrayed his humor, and Mathias found himself wanting more. The man he was talking to now bore little resemblance to the dour person he had met the last time Pascal came in.

"No, but I want an honest opinion of it," Mathias said. "I'll tell you what's in it after you tell me if you like it. It's a new recipe Michel is trying, so it's not on the menu yet. Adrien said he could try it on some customers to see if we should add it to the menu."

"Updating the menu is always a risk and a challenge in one," Pascal agreed. Mathias wanted to ask where Pascal worked or had worked to have that kind of insight, but he didn't want to be too forward.

Pascal took a sip of the drink, his face showing the depth of his consideration. Again Mathias was struck by the sense of talking with someone who knew what he was doing, someone who did these kinds of things and made these kinds of decisions regularly.

"It's interesting," Pascal said. "A hint of sweetness from the pear, but not sugary, and there's something else there as well. This isn't just a cosmo with pear substituted for the cranberry. What else is in it?"

"Elderflower cordial," Mathias said. "It's not a common ingredient, at least not that I've seen since I started working here. You'd probably know more than I would."

Pascal shook his head. "I know wines well, but I don't pay a lot of attention to liqueurs. I try all the new drinks on the menu at work so I know what a drink tastes like if someone asks, but most of my patrons order wine rather than cocktails, outside of a few standards."

"Where do you work, if you don't mind me asking?" Mathias asked.

"La Colombe d'Or," Pascal replied. "I've worked there for the past nineteen years."

"I've seen it as I walk by," Mathias said. "It seems like a really nice place."

"It is," Pascal said.

"Mathias!"

Mathias looked away to see Adrien gesturing for him. "Oops. The boss is calling."

Pascal smiled. "Don't let him yell at you too much. Tell him I was monopolizing your time."

Mathias smiled all the way over to the owner of Le Salon.

"You seem to have hit it off with Pascal," Adrien said, "but don't forget you have other tables besides his."

"Sorry," Mathias said. "Michel made a new drink, and Pascal was testing it out for us. I wanted to see what he thought."

"Just don't neglect your other customers," Adrien repeated.

Mathias nodded and ignored his impulse to return to Pascal's table. He made his rounds, smiling at the patrons flirtatiously, making sure to bend and stretch just the right way so they could ogle him to their heart's content. He ignored the wandering hands at table eight. The man groped his ass but didn't try to go beyond that, and Mathias had seen him more than once. He was handsy, but he tipped really well, so Mathias figured he could put up with the indignity.

By the time he made it back around to Pascal's table, the two men from the other night had joined him, and Pascal had retreated into his shell. Mathias tried to draw him out, but the more he flirted, the more withdrawn Pascal got. Mathias almost gave up, but Pascal's glass was empty. Rather than take the risk, he got a vodka martini from Michel and brought it to Pascal. "Our treat, for helping us out with the new drink."

Pascal smiled again, and Mathias returned it instantly, relieved to see the genuine expression on his face again instead of the slightly forced one he'd given Mathias when he'd first come back to the table.

He figured that was as good as he was going to get with Pascal's friends there—he hoped they were his friends and not his lovers—so he let it go at that and went back to the other tables with a bounce in his step and a smile on his face.

CHAPTER 3

PASCAL HAD never been so grateful for a night off as he was a little over a week later. His fridge was empty (thus the plethora of bags in his arms), his apartment was a disaster area, and he desperately needed to do laundry.

He made it to the door of the apartment building and muffled a curse. His keys were in his back pocket, and with his hands full, he couldn't reach them. He'd either have to set down all the bags or wait for someone to open the door. At this hour of the day, it might not be a long wait, but he didn't want his milk or meat to spoil.

"Here, hold on just a minute. I'll get the door for you."

Pascal let out the breath he'd been holding in a sigh of relief. "Thank you," he said automatically before turning to see which of his neighbors had come to his rescue. He didn't know everyone in his building, given that his work schedule didn't always leave him free to socialize at the same time as someone who worked normal hours, but he knew more than half of them, in passing if not more.

It took Pascal a minute to place the young man walking toward him as the waiter from Le Salon, the one who had flirted with René and Benjamin but had actually talked to Pascal. Instead of wearing form-fitting jeans and a tight T-shirt, he was wearing a suit. Not the fanciest or most elegant one Pascal had ever seen. Not even the nicest one he'd seen this week, but a nice enough one that it was a sharp contrast to the vision that had filled Pascal's personal time over the past week. What little of it he'd had.

"Looking good…." He cast around for the kid's name. "Mathias. That's your name, right?"

"Yes," Mathias said with a smile. "I guess I should have actually introduced myself at some point, eh? Mathias Perras."

"Pascal Larocque. You're not dressed for an evening waiting tables," Pascal observed as Mathias fished his keys out of a very nice briefcase.

"I work at BMO during the day," Mathias explained. "The bar is just a way to earn a little extra money." He held the door for Pascal. As soon as they got inside, Mathias reached for the bags encumbering Pascal's hands. "Let me take one or two of those. I don't know which apartment is yours, but you'll never make it up the stairs with your arms full like that."

Pascal turned over a couple of the bags, relieved not to have quite as much weight to carry, and led Mathias up the four flights of stairs to his apartment. Usually he viewed the climb as a bit of extra exercise, but after the week he'd had and with the load of groceries in his arms, it was just one more annoyance. "Why did I think living on the top floor was a good idea?" he grumbled.

"Because it has the best view?" Mathias asked from behind him.

"Because it has washer and dryer attachments in the apartment," Pascal replied, feeling a smile forming.

"Oh, now I'm jealous!" Mathias said. "I have to take my suits to the cleaners, of course, but it would be nice not to have to take my jeans and stuff to the Laundromat. Such a pain in the ass!"

"When I got the job at la Colombe d'Or and could afford a nicer apartment than the dingy hole in the wall I had before, I swore I'd never live in another place that didn't have a washer and dryer," Pascal admitted. They reached the landing for his floor, and he set the groceries down. Mathias had let him in the front door, but Pascal needed his keys to open the door. "Thank you for your help."

"It's not a problem. I can help you get them inside if you want."

Pascal almost said no, thank you. He was already at his door, and even if he made two or three trips to carry the bags inside, it was far different than having to make two or three trips up the stairs. Then again, if he said yes, he'd be able to spend a few more minutes with this other side of Mathias. He'd tried to avoid staring, but the kid could carry off a suit!

"Thanks. If you're sure you don't mind."

"Not at all." Mathias grabbed another of the bags as Pascal picked up the others and carried them inside. Fortunately most of the mess in his apartment was confined to the bedroom, primarily because he hadn't been home long enough to do more than toss his dirty clothes aside as he fell into bed. The floor could afford to be swept, but he didn't have a pile of dirty dishes stacked in the sink or anything else grossly offensive in the visible part of his apartment, so he wasn't too embarrassed to have Mathias see it.

"You can just set them on the counter," Pascal said. "I'll get them put away. Can I offer you a beer?"

He'd made the offer impulsively, but as soon as the words were out, he was glad of them. Mathias at the bar had been attractive enough. Mathias in a suit was enough to push all of Pascal's buttons. Not that he actually thought Mathias would be interested in someone like him, especially not if he had a career planned at the Banque de Montréal, but it couldn't hurt to get to know him a little better.

Mathias looked down at his watch, his lips contorting as he read the time. "I wish I could, but I have half an hour to shower, change, and get to Le Salon if I don't want to be late for my shift."

"Another time, then," Pascal said. "I don't want to make you late."

"Another time, I'll take you up on it," Mathias said with a smile. "I think I'm off on Tuesday."

Pascal frowned. "I work on Tuesday night. What about Saturday? What time do you have to be at the bar?"

"Not until three, but I already made plans with a friend from work. I have to go now, but come by the bar if you have time. We'll figure something out when I bring you a drink."

Pascal smiled and nodded automatically, even though he hadn't made any plans to go out that night. Then again, he hadn't planned on running into Mathias outside his building either. "I'm going to make dinner first," he said. "I don't want to drink on an empty stomach, but I'll come by later."

Mathias's smile lit up the room. "Great! I'll see you there. I've got to run now."

Pascal accompanied him back to the door and watched him walk down the hall and down the stairs. When Mathias was out of sight, he went back inside and shut the door, barely resisting the urge to pound his head against the wall. What was he thinking, lusting over a kid like Mathias? He hadn't asked Mathias how old he was, but everything about him proclaimed he was fresh out of university, just starting his career. If Pascal was lucky, Mathias was twenty-four or twenty-five, only half

Pascal's age, instead of twenty-two or twenty-three, and even less than half Pascal's age. Regardless, he had no business inviting him in for a beer or anything else. He had been called many things in his life. He refused to add "dirty old man" to the list.

AN HOUR and a quick dinner later (Pascal pretended he hadn't put off cooking the chowder he'd planned to reheat all week so he could go to Le Salon), Pascal walked into the bar, glancing around in search of Mathias so he could sit at a table in the younger man's area. All his doubts and guilt from earlier rushed back, but he focused on the fact that Mathias had asked him to come by, had seemed interested in finding a time when they could have a beer, maybe a meal, and some conversation. Maybe it wouldn't be anything more than Mathias picking his brain for suggestions about his schedule or getting better tips, or moving to a better paid position, but whatever the conversation ended up being, Mathias had been as interested in it happening as Pascal was.

"Bonsoir, Pascal," Mathias said as he came to the table. "What are you drinking tonight?"

"Does your bartender have another of those pear drinks you brought me last time? It was pretty good."

"One pear martini, coming right up," Mathias said with a grin Pascal couldn't quite decipher. He smiled and flirted with all his customers. All the servers did. It guaranteed them better tips, and that was the bulk of their income, just as it was for Pascal. The difference was the size of the tips. At la Colombe d'Or, a party of two routinely left a twenty-dollar tip or more. A large party could leave as much as a hundred, and Pascal served eight to ten parties a night, not counting the lunch shift. Here at Le Salon, Mathias probably did well to earn five dollars a table unless they stayed all night or were a large party. Fifty or a hundred bucks in tips a night was Pascal's spare change. If a smile or a bit of flirting earned him a few more dollars, Pascal could hardly blame him. He just wished he didn't feel like Mathias's smile for him was the same as the one he gave everyone else. Yes, he was a customer at the bar, and yes, he'd be leaving Mathias a nice tip when he left, but he didn't need to be flirted with or seduced into giving one. He wanted more than that. He wanted the bank employee he'd met in his apartment building an hour ago. That didn't look likely, though, so Pascal resigned himself to the torture of watching Mathias flirt with everyone else.

"So Saturday won't work," Mathias said without preamble as he set the martini down in front of Pascal. "What about Sunday?"

"It's my week to have lunch with my parents and do their shopping and everything," Pascal said. "They're in their eighties and shut in. My sister and I alternate weeks, and it's my turn. I'd see if she could switch, but we had to switch two weeks ago, so she's already gone two Sundays in a row. She needs a Sunday to spend with her kid."

"Well, damn," Mathias said. "I guess that leaves a week from Saturday. If you're free, I mean."

"The restaurant is closed for lunch on the weekends," Pascal said. "Not enough foot traffic in that area of town to make it worth staying open. In the evenings, yes, but not for lunch. Our lunch traffic is almost all people working in the surrounding buildings, and all those offices are closed on the weekends. So I'm pretty much always free on Saturday unless I decide to do something with René and Benjamin before I head in for the dinner shift."

Before Mathias could say anything else, one of the other servers walked by and bumped Mathias with his shoulder. "Adrien's frowning at you. You need to check on your other tables."

"Allez," Pascal said. "I don't want to get you in trouble with your boss."

Mathias flashed another smile and left Pascal to waltz over to another table. A moment later, Adrien came over. "Was he bothering you?"

"No, not at all," Pascal replied. "We live in the same building. We were just chatting a bit."

That didn't seem to appease Adrien the way Pascal had hoped it would.

"I'm not so sure about that one. He's cute enough and the customers seem to like him, but he's flighty. I keep having to remind him of things. They all flirt to some extent, but he's pushing it. I don't mind a little flirting, but I won't have them trying to pick up my customers."

"He isn't, or at least not with me." If anything, Pascal had been trying to pick up Mathias, not the other way around. He hadn't seen anything wrong with coming out tonight so he could talk to Mathias a little more, but if it was going to get him in trouble with his boss,

Pascal would have to reconsider that plan. If Mathias lost his job because of Pascal, that certainly wouldn't endear him to the younger man. Maybe he'd had the right of it earlier tonight after all. Maybe he was bad for Mathias. "I don't know him all that well, but he seems like a good kid. He works another job besides this one. Give him a break. He's already worked a full day when he comes in here at night."

"My customers deserve good service, no matter what's going on in their server's life," Adrien said.

"Yes, and I'm not saying you should let him get away with bad service, but he's certainly never given me bad service, and you know how picky I am."

The best part of that was that it was true. Mathias might be inexperienced and maybe a little overenthusiastic, but he didn't give bad service. He'd found a new drink for Pascal, convinced René to try something new as well, and had generally made their past few visits to Le Salon enjoyable ones. Even if nothing else came of his interest in Mathias, he would miss the younger man's smile if Adrien let him go.

"I'll give him another warning, then," Adrien said. "Good help is hard to find. If he's giving good service, I suppose it's worth coaching him on the rest."

"I'll stop monopolizing him," Pascal said. "I know better than most how hard his job is."

"It's still his responsibility to balance everything, not yours."

Pascal couldn't argue with that, but he could make sure he wasn't making Mathias's job harder than it needed to be. "I'm not asking you to do him any favors, but remember how hard it was when you were first starting out. Give him the benefit of the doubt."

Adrien winked at Pascal. "Only because he's cute and you asked."

Pascal couldn't argue that, but it worried him at the same time. Had he put Mathias's job that much at risk? If he had, he couldn't keep coming by himself on his nights off as an excuse to see Mathias. He'd never forgive himself if his presence cost Mathias his job, and while he wasn't sure he wanted to pursue a relationship with Mathias (assuming Mathias was even interested in such a thing), he wouldn't stand a chance if Mathias lost his job because of Pascal.

"Whatever you're thinking that put that frown on your face, stop right now."

Pascal looked up and smiled before he realized what he was doing. "You shouldn't spend too much time with me. You have other customers too. You don't want to make Adrien annoyed with you."

"Adrien is always annoyed with me," Mathias admitted. "Talking to you isn't going to change that."

"Not talking to me might help."

"No, then he'd say I was neglecting you and be annoyed because of that."

"I could sit at someone else's table," Pascal suggested.

"Then I'd be distracted because I was jealous of whoever got the chance to flirt with you."

"I think that's a conversation best saved for a week from Saturday," Pascal said after a moment. He wasn't at all sure how he felt about Mathias's casual declaration, but he knew this was neither the time nor the place to discuss it, not with Adrien hovering in the background somewhere and the sense of necessity that overshadowed all of Mathias's actions here, where his flirting could be as much about a tip as about anything else. Pascal wanted the bank employee, not the bar boy.

"Next Saturday it is," Mathias said, "although I hope you'll come in and see me between now and then."

"That will depend on my schedule," Pascal equivocated. "I don't want to make promises I might not be able to keep."

Mathias frowned, clearly not happy with that answer. "Give me your phone."

Frowning in confusion, Pascal pulled out his phone and handed it to Mathias. Mathias typed in a number and waited for a minute. "There. Now you have my number and I have yours. So we can make plans for Saturday."

CHAPTER 4

"HAVE YOU seen your dreamboat again?" Louis asked Mathias when they had the same lunch break the following Tuesday.

"Not just saw him," Mathias said with a grin. "Talked to him and got his number and a lunch date on Saturday."

"Nice." Louis grinned back. "So tell me about him."

"His name's Pascal. He works at la Colombe d'Or. He lives on the fourth floor of my building."

"I'm supposed to have lunch with Mr. Belanger next week. He usually wants to go to la Colombe d'Or. Maybe I'll see him."

"He's in his forties, dark hair with a bit of gray at the temples, but absolutely gorgeous. You can't miss him."

"I'll look for him," Louis said. "I want a face to go with the name. Have you considered how you're going to make this work if both of you have restaurant schedules? He's not going to have a lot of nights off."

"That's why we have a lunch date," Mathias said. "It's the one day and time neither of us has other commitments, at least not this week. Let's see how that goes before you try to marry me off."

Louis laughed. "Is that what I was doing? I thought I was just giving you the benefit of my vast experience?"

"*Vast* experience?" Mathias teased. "Careful there or I'm going to end up thinking the wrong thing."

Louis kicked him under the table. "That's not what I meant. You're burning the candle at both ends. I just don't want to see you light a fire in the middle as well, or there'll be nothing left."

"It's just temporary," Mathias said. "Once the training period is over, I'll get a salary increase, and that should be enough to let me cut back on the hours I work at the bar. That'll give me more time for myself and for Pascal, if things work out."

"Any particular reason why they wouldn't?"

"He's so far out of my league," Mathias said. "I'm a green kid, and he's…."

"He's probably sitting at home thinking he's too old for you," Louis said when Mathias didn't finish his sentence. "I'm not saying there isn't an age difference or a difference in experience or anything else. I'm just saying don't write yourself off. Whose idea was lunch?"

Mathias had to stop and think for a minute. "His, I guess. I helped him carry his groceries up last Thursday. His hands were full. He offered me a beer, but I didn't have time. I was going to be late for my shift at the bar, so he suggested we do it some other time. The decision to have lunch was a bit of a negotiation of schedules, but the initial idea was his."

"Then he's got that much interest in you," Louis said. "You'll have to hold his interest, but you've managed to catch it. That's a good start."

"I suppose you're right," Mathias replied slowly. "Thanks, Louis. It's easy to lose perspective."

"That's what I'm here for," Louis said. "Lunchtime's over. Back to work."

PASCAL MET Benjamin for lunch on Wednesday when he had the day off. He tried to meet one or both of his friends on his day off when he could, and since he hadn't seen them on his last day off, he'd been determined not to miss them again.

"Bonjour," Benjamin said as he joined Pascal at the table.

"Bonjour," Pascal replied. "How are you today?"

"Very well. How are you?"

Pascal debated how to answer that. Benjamin didn't tease him as badly as René did, but anything he told Benjamin, René would know before long.

"Pascal?" Benjamin prompted.

Pascal bit back a curse. He'd obviously waited too long to answer. "I'm well," he said. "I… I might have a date on Saturday."

"I thought you were working on Saturday," Benjamin said.

"For lunch," Pascal clarified. "His schedule is as crazy as mine. That was the only time we were both free for the next two weeks."

Benjamin cocked his eyebrow at Pascal. "If he's that busy—and I know how busy you are—is this a good idea?"

"I already know it's a bad idea," Pascal said. "That hasn't seemed to stop me."

The waiter arrived to take their order, forestalling the questions Pascal could see in Benjamin's eyes. When they were alone again, Benjamin fixed him with a pointed stare. "So why is it a bad idea?"

"He's practically a kid," Pascal said. "He works at the BMO during the day and at Le Salon in the evenings because he wants to live on rue Sainte-Catherine and can't afford it on his bank salary alone. He doesn't have time for a relationship, I don't want a random hookup, but I don't see how anything lasting can come from it."

"Then why are you having lunch with him, then?" Benjamin asked.

"Because I'm only human," Pascal said, "and he's young and gorgeous and for whatever reason he's interested in me right now. It's one hell of an ego boost, even if it doesn't last."

"Don't doom yourself to failure because you don't believe you can succeed," Benjamin advised. "You may be right and it might not last, but you could be wrong. If he's willing to give it a chance, do yourself a favor and give it everything you have too. Don't ruin it by holding back."

"So instead I'll scare him away by being too eager," Pascal countered.

"Just be yourself," Benjamin said with a huff. "You're being deliberately dense."

"He's half my age," Pascal replied. "I'd say I passed dense and entered the realm of insane some time ago."

Benjamin rolled his eyes. "You said he works at Le Salon. Which one is he?"

"The brunet with the spiky blond tips and tight jeans."

"They all wear tight jeans," Benjamin retorted. "It's part of their charm."

Pascal laughed. "The one with the really tight jeans."

Benjamin grinned. "Oh, *that* one. Good taste, old man."

"You're three months younger than I am. Who are you calling old?"

"Which means you'll always be older than I am," Benjamin replied. Pascal shook his head as he bit back a laugh. "There's more to life than your age," Benjamin continued more seriously, "and more to age than a number. I've known men our age with all the maturity of a two-year-old and kids barely out of their teens with old souls. You're a very young forty-eight. If he's mature for his age, there might not be as much difference as you think."

Pascal wasn't convinced, but he could see the logic in Benjamin's words. He wasn't ready to jump in with both feet, but he could test the waters and see what developed.

DESPITE HIS better judgment, Pascal let Benjamin and René talk him into going to Le Salon on Thursday. He'd worked the lunch shift but had the evening off, so he didn't have an excuse, and honestly, he wanted to see Mathias again, to see if the chemistry continued. Meeting at the bar when Mathias was working wouldn't give them a lot of chance to interact because Mathias had to work, and Pascal didn't want to give Adrien a reason to speak with him again. He'd be able to see Mathias, though, and that outweighed the rest of his concerns. They would sit at a table with another server so he could just watch Mathias across the room, even if that made him feel somewhere between a stalker and a high school kid hanging out near his crush's next class just to catch a glimpse of him in the halls. Hopefully Mathias would either err on the side of sweet or simply chalk it up to Pascal and his friends being regulars at the bar.

He made sure to arrive early enough that he'd get to pick the table, deliberately choosing one in a section where a different waiter was taking orders. He didn't see Mathias, but that worked in his favor, actually. If Mathias asked why Pascal wasn't at one of Mathias's tables, Pascal could honestly say he hadn't known which tables were Mathias's when he came in.

René arrived before Benjamin, greeting Pascal without any unusual teasing, making Pascal wonder if Benjamin hadn't said anything about their lunch conversation after all. It would be surprising, but maybe Benjamin had developed some discretion since the last time Pascal had confided in him.

They chatted idly until the waiter came up to take their order. René flirted as he always did, bantering back and forth with the waiter as he decided on a drink. Pascal ordered a vodka martini. He'd save trying new drinks for Mathias.

"Not feeling adventurous tonight?" René asked when the server left.

"No one to be adventurous for," Pascal replied without thinking.

"Oh, I was right!" René said. "Benjamin owes me ten bucks. You are interested in the new kid."

That explained Benjamin's reticence. So much for discretion. "That remains to be seen," Pascal replied. "It doesn't do much good if he's not interested in return."

"He was all over you last time."

"He's all over all his customers," Pascal said. He didn't need to look in Mathias's direction to know he was flirting with the table of twentysomethings that had come in while they were giving their order. He could hear the laughter from across the bar. "Ask me on Sunday, and we'll see where things stand."

René stared at him for a minute before grinning widely. "You dog. You have a date."

"For lunch," Pascal verified. "And no, you can't come over Saturday afternoon to see how it went, and furthermore, you can't come to the restaurant Saturday night. You can call Sunday afternoon after I get home from Maman's."

"I thought you were at your mother's last weekend."

"I was. Sylvie and I switched weeks, so now I have two weekends in a row."

"Fine, so I'll call you between three and five on Sunday. Or do you have to go in early this weekend?"

"No, it's my weekend to close. Someone else gets to open," Pascal replied.

Benjamin joined them then.

"Pay up," René said by way of greeting. "He's got a date. That counts as being interested."

Benjamin flushed and handed René the money. "For the record," Benjamin said to René, "I didn't discourage him, even if it meant losing the bet." He turned toward Pascal. "I didn't think you'd be interested, but now that you are, I want you to be happy."

"We'll see," Pascal said. "It's way too soon to be talking like that."

"Why are we sitting all the way over here when he's over there?" Benjamin asked.

"Because the last time I was here, he got in trouble with Adrien for paying too much attention to me and not enough to his other customers," Pascal said. "I didn't want to do that to him again."

"We could have gone somewhere else," René offered.

"Yeah, but then I wouldn't even get to see him."

"Man, you've got it *bad*," René teased. Pascal flushed. "I'm glad. You've been alone long enough. Robert wouldn't want you to mourn forever."

"It's not just that," Pascal said. "I've had it all, you know. It's hard to imagine getting a second chance at that kind of love and harder still to imagine settling for anything less."

"That's fine," Benjamin said, "but remember this too: you're not the man you were then. Don't expect a new partner or a new relationship to be like the old one. Find a partner who gives you what you need now, not who can give you what Robert gave you."

"What's that supposed to mean?" Pascal demanded.

Benjamin sighed. "You met him when you were in your twenties. You had a few good years together before he got sick, and then you spent the rest of his life taking care of him as cancer stole his health and eventually his life. You're a different man than you were then. I'm not saying you didn't love him, and I'm certainly not saying he didn't love you, but you don't need another Robert. You need someone for the man you are now, not the man you were then."

"And you think Mathias is that man?"

"I haven't the slightest idea," Benjamin said with a bright smile, "but *you* seem to be entertaining the idea, and I know you too well. You'll do your best to talk yourself out of it if René and I don't knock some sense into you, so consider yourself knocked."

Mathias came up behind Pascal before he could reply and set Pascal's and René's drinks on the table. "Hi, guys," he said with a smile. "Your server went on break, so I said I'd drop these off and take any additional orders."

Benjamin ordered a beer while looking pointedly at Pascal. Pascal smiled up at Mathias, who smiled back. "I'm glad I got a chance to say hi," Mathias added. "I can't stay over here long. I've got customers to take care of, but I'm looking forward to Saturday."

"Me too," Pascal said, not sure whether to be impressed that Mathias seemed to be taking his job much more seriously or discouraged that Mathias found him much easier to resist than he had the last time Pascal came into the bar. The brush of Mathias's fingers across the back of his neck settled his doubts and left Pascal wishing it was Saturday right now.

Ignoring the smirks of his friends, Pascal caught Mathias's fingers and squeezed lightly. "You want to bring me a new drink?" he asked. "Something… different?"

Mathias's smile lit up the whole bar. "I'll get right on it."

CHAPTER 5

PASCAL WOKE up far earlier on Saturday than he would usually be awake. La Colombe d'Or stayed open until midnight on Friday, and then they had to prepare everything for Saturday, so Pascal rarely got home before 2:00 a.m. What had possessed him to invite Mathias to his place for lunch instead of meeting him somewhere, Pascal couldn't say, but he regretted it now. He hadn't had time to go shopping, and he hadn't wanted to come across as pretentious by bringing something home from work and reheating it. He ate more meals at la Colombe d'Or than he did at home since he didn't want to put the time and effort into cooking for himself, but this wasn't a meal for himself. This was a date with Mathias, and since he'd invited the man over, he needed to make an effort to actually feed him. Fortunately, at the height of summer, he could find plenty of fresh vegetables at the market at Place Pasteur. With a little bit of effort, he could whip up a dressing for a pasta salad. He had a nice rosé wine he could stick in the fridge to chill and plenty of beer if Mathias preferred that to wine.

He tugged on a reasonably clean T-shirt and a pair of shorts for the trip to the market. He could take a shower and change into something nicer after he was done cooking. As long as he didn't run into Mathias in the halls this morning, he'd be fine.

The sky was so blue it hurt to look at it when he walked outside. He winced and pulled on his sunglasses. He loved the sky like that, but not when he was running on too little sleep and not enough caffeine. He'd have to remedy that before Mathias came over or he wouldn't be pleasant company. He wasn't convinced Benjamin was right and that things could work between Mathias and him, but he wasn't going to shoot himself in the foot either.

The street was quiet this early almost until he reached the market. Saturday mornings along rue Sainte-Catherine were dead except for people who wanted what the market had to offer. Everyone else was still in bed, sleeping off the partying from the night before. It made for an incredibly vibrant nightlife, something Pascal didn't get to take advantage of as much as he wanted since he was at the restaurant more nights than not, but it also meant he never had to worry about coming home late, because everyone else was up just as late. On Saturday, though, most people didn't stir before noon. He couldn't remember the last time he'd been awake this early on a Saturday.

When he arrived at the market, he decided on a quick tour through the stalls to see what his choices were before he bought. He was a decent cook with enough time and the right ingredients, even if he didn't usually bother with it. Today, though, he was determined to find the right ingredients.

Having finished his rounds, he decided on a mixture of squashes and peppers that could be sliced thinly and eaten raw along with some beautiful ripe tomatoes. Armed with his provisions, he headed back toward home.

"This is getting to be a habit." Mathias's voice started Pascal as he neared the door to their building.

"Mathias. I didn't expect to see you so early this morning."

"I usually go for a run when I get up on Saturdays," Mathias explained. "It's pretty much the only time I get any exercise with my schedule the way it is. Of course I usually get up a lot later on Saturdays, but I have plans for today." The wink that accompanied his words went straight to Pascal's head, his whole body tingling with it.

"What a coincidence," Pascal said, determined to keep his wits about him in the face of Mathias's flirting. He wasn't a teenager to lose his head at the first sign of interest from a pretty face. A very attractively flushed and sweaty face right at the moment, to go with a very attractively buff and sweaty body. He took in the loose, sweat-damp T-shirt and clingy running shorts with a swift glance. He could linger over the memory later, when he was alone and less likely to embarrass himself. "I was just doing some shopping to facilitate my plans as well."

Mathias peeked into the bag Pascal carried. "Looks like quite a feast. Someone's trying to make a good impression."

Pascal flushed despite himself. "Nothing wrong with taking pride in a well-prepared meal," he said defensively as they walked inside the building.

"Nothing at all," Mathias agreed. "Good luck with your *plans*."

Pascal cursed under his breath all the way up the stairs to his apartment. So much for not shooting himself in the foot. He hadn't shaved or showered, he was dressed in old ratty clothes without the gym as an excuse for it, and he'd come off sounding like an idiot while he was talking to Mathias. He'd be lucky if Mathias even showed up after this.

With a sigh, he pulled out a pan and put water on to boil for the pasta and then set to chopping up the vegetables he'd bought at the market. It was mindless work, which was good because all his energy was currently focused on replaying the conversation in his mind and trying to figure out what he could have said differently. He'd finished the zucchini and was washing the squash when his phone chimed to let him know he had a text.

Should I bring anything for lunch?

Pascal considered the question for a minute. He had the pasta salad and drinks. He didn't really have any kind of dessert, though. *Only if you want something sweet for dessert.*

I already know what I want for dessert.

Pascal stared at the reply, entirely unsure of how to interpret it. He could read plenty into it with no effort whatsoever, but that didn't mean Mathias intended the innuendo. Then again, he was an intelligent young man to have gotten a job working at the Banque de Montréal, so surely he knew how it *could* be interpreted, even if that wasn't what he actually meant by it. If he actually had a dessert in mind, Pascal would feel like an idiot for replying to the innuendo, but if he was really proposing what it sounded like he was proposing, Pascal needed to put a stop to it. He hadn't invited Mathias to lunch as a prelude for a quick tumble between the sheets. He wasn't interested in fucking Mathias—okay, that was a lie. He'd like nothing more than to take Mathias to bed and spend hours there, but he wasn't *only* interested in fucking him. He debated a moment more and then typed back, *Then bring it with you.*

If Mathias really had a dessert in mind, that answer wouldn't give away where Pascal's mind had gone, and if he'd been flirting, well, maybe it would help tone things down a bit. Pascal wasn't a prude. He didn't take issue with sex, even just for sex's sake, but he was past the age of thinking with his dick. He wanted more than that, and maybe he couldn't have more with Mathias, but he wasn't going to ruin his chances by starting with no-strings sex.

Mathias didn't reply right away, which worried Pascal a little, but he couldn't do anything about it now. If his text had been the wrong answer, he'd deal with it when Mathias came for lunch.

He assembled the pasta salad quickly and put it in the fridge to chill, then went to take a shower and make himself presentable. It was already getting warm in the apartment even with the windows open, so he took as quick a shower as he could so he wouldn't add steam to the heat already building up. When he was done, he dressed in his lightest linen trousers and a loose button-down shirt. His sister had insisted the forest-green fabric brought out the blue in his changeable eyes when he wore it. Pascal didn't know about that, but it was light and comfortable, two requirements on a warm summer day in a fourth-floor apartment with no air-conditioning.

He did a quick pass through his apartment to make sure everything was presentable. Fortunately, he was relatively neat by nature, so other than putting away the previous day's mail that he'd been too tired to deal with the night before, he didn't have much to do to get ready.

When everything was done but the waiting, he picked up his laptop and forced himself to focus on a search for new books. When his ladies had come for their monthly visit last time, Hélène had mentioned a new book, but she hadn't said when it would be released. Pascal searched for her name, refusing to be embarrassed when it popped up on autofill. His date with Mathias notwithstanding, he had little enough romance in his life. He refused to apologize for wanting it in his fiction. Besides, Hélène was one of his ladies. Pascal St-Laurent had been born soon after Robert's death in a joking attempt to make him smile again. He hadn't expected anything to come of it when he gave permission for them to use his name and likeness in one of their books. He'd certainly never expected it to turn into the series one reviewer had named the James Bond for the twenty-first century, but when Martine brought him the first book, he'd had to fight back tears. His ladies had done so much for him. The least he could do was buy their books. He had signed copies of every single one each of them had written, even the ones from before he knew them, and he didn't intend to have a gap now just because he was distracted by a potential date.

He'd just completed his search for anything new Nicole had out, in case she'd neglected to mention it (she did that a lot. He relied on the other three to tell him when she had a release) when a knock on the door interrupted him. He saved his order and went to answer the door.

"I'm a little early," Mathias said, although the clock on Pascal's computer had said exactly eleven thirty, the time they'd agreed on. "I hope you don't mind."

"Not at all," Pascal said. "I was just buying some books."

"You like to read?" Mathias asked as he came inside. Pascal took the bakery box Mathias handed him, relieved to see an actual dessert. It could have been a cover to explain the texts when Pascal didn't reply flirtatiously to the last one, but it could also mean Mathias had really been talking about dessert.

"Yes, mostly on my Kindle these days since it's so easy to carry, but I buy some books in print no matter what."

Pascal carried the dessert into the kitchen and came back out to find Mathias browsing through the bookshelf where he kept his ladies' books. "This is quite a collection. I'm sensing a trend here."

"They're friends," Pascal said. "I've read all of them, so I'm not just buying them because they're my friends, but that's why they're in print, not e-book."

"Wait, you know the author of the Pascal St-Laurent books?" Mathias said, pointing to the spines of that series.

"Martine and the other three as well, yes. I met them at the restaurant," Pascal said. "They come in once a month. I've known them for years."

"Do you think…? No, that's silly."

"Do I think what?" Pascal prompted. "It doesn't hurt to ask."

"I was going to ask if you could get her autograph for me," Mathias said. "I know she has millions of fans, probably, but when I first realized I was gay, I read a couple of her books, not the Pascal St-Laurent ones, but some of the others, and it really helped me feel more at ease with myself."

"I can do that," Pascal said, "but she'd love to hear your story herself. I have her e-mail, and I know she reads and answers all her own fan mail. She'll sometimes talk about the ones that really touch her when she comes in. They all do."

"That's just so cool," Mathias said. He looked so young in that moment that Pascal's heart hurt just staring at him. He'd seen Mathias the waiter and Mathias the banker, but this was just Mathias, no roles, no façades. Pascal wanted to see more of him. "So do they... I don't know... tell you about their books and stuff? I mean when they're writing them," Mathias continued.

"Sometimes," Pascal said, "but they're never my only table, remember, so while they may talk books and plots and problems and everything else, most of that is to each other, not to me. Every once in a while, they'll ask my opinion to get a male perspective on something, especially if they disagree on it, but for the most part, it's more like just mentioning they have a new book coming out or they got something accepted or that kind of thing. No real details."

"Still... do you know when the next Pascal St-Laurent book is coming out?"

"Not for sure, but Martine said she was trying for one every six months, so that would be another four months. Why? Do you want to know what happens?"

"Of course I do," Mathias said. "I heard Jack finally divorced his wife, not that I've had time to read recently. I'm dying to know if Pascal makes a move now that Jack's free."

Pascal laughed. "No, I don't know if he does or not. I do know there will be at least two more because she mentioned working on a new one now, and with her schedule, the one that'll come out in four months is already complete."

Mathias grinned. "Good." He shook himself a bit, and his smile took on a slightly more flirtatious edge. "Sorry for the geek moment there. I've met other fans before, but never anyone who knows the author."

"It's fine," Pascal said. "I don't mind." He couldn't help but wonder what Mathias would say if he knew Pascal wasn't just a friend of the author but the model for the character, but he didn't volunteer that information. It was too tied up with Robert's death, something he didn't share easily. If things worked out between him and Mathias, he'd have to talk about Robert eventually, but not on the first date. "Would you like something to drink? I've got a rosé that's cold or there's beer."

"I'm usually more of a beer drinker," Mathias admitted, "so maybe I should expand my palate."

"A glass of wine, then?" Pascal confirmed. When Mathias nodded, Pascal went back into the kitchen and returned with the bottle, two glasses, and a corkscrew. If he opened the bottle with a little more flourish than strictly necessary, Mathias certainly wasn't any the wiser.

He poured a sip into one of the glasses. "Do you want to do the honors?"

"So that isn't just for show?" Mathias asked.

"No," Pascal said. "Sure, people play it up to make themselves look sophisticated, and part of it is about appreciating the full aesthetics of a wine, not just guzzling it down, but sometimes a bottle of wine goes bad, and the only way to realize that is by smelling and tasting it. Better a little sip than a huge mouthful if it isn't good."

"Yeah, but I wouldn't know if it was good or not," Mathias said.

"Taste it," Pascal said. "You'll either like it or you won't. If you like it, I'll pour you some more. If you don't, I'll get you a beer. Even if it hasn't gone bad, if you don't like it, you shouldn't drink it."

Mathias took a sip obediently. His face didn't curl up in disgust, so Pascal took that as a good sign.

"This is pretty good." Mathias held his glass out for more.

"It's a nice summer wine," Pascal agreed. "Perfect for a hot day and a cold salad. Take your wine outside. I'll get the salad and join you."

Mathias shook his head. "You made lunch. At least let me help you set the table and carry everything outside."

"You don't have to," Pascal said, but he didn't try to stop Mathias from following him into the kitchen. He had the plates and silverware set out, so it was just a matter of gathering them, the pasta salad from the refrigerator, and the wine, and carrying them outside, but Pascal couldn't have gotten it all in one trip without a tray from the restaurant, which he didn't keep at home.

The balcony, when they stepped out onto it, was about the size of a postage stamp, with just enough room for a little café table, two chairs, and a flower box on the railing, but Pascal couldn't imagine staying inside on a day like this. The balcony faced northwest so it was still slightly shaded from the sun, but it gave them a view of Mont Royal off to the left.

"Your view is much nicer than mine," Mathias said as they set the table.

"Which way does your apartment face?" Pascal asked.

"Into the alley. I have a balcony if you want to call it that, but I'm not sure I'd want to use it even if I was home often enough to take advantage of it."

"Ah. Yes, I can see that not being enjoyable," Pascal said. "You're welcome to take advantage of mine today. What time do you have to be at Le Salon?"

"At four," Mathias said. "Do you have to work tonight?"

"Yes, but I don't have to be there until five," Pascal said. "I worked until closing last night, so I don't have to be there until we open tonight. The people who had the earlier shift will have to come in and do all the setup today."

Pascal served the pasta salad and poured more wine into Mathias's glass before lifting his own in a silent toast. Mathias clinked their glasses together. "To a wonderful summer afternoon."

And many more. Pascal didn't voice the thought. Everything was going well, and he didn't want to jinx it.

CHAPTER 6

"I'M GLAD we actually have some time today," Mathias said when Pascal didn't answer his toast in words. He didn't think he'd crossed the line with the sentiment, but Pascal had already proven oddly sensitive about certain things, so Mathias wasn't going to press his luck.

"Me too," Pascal said. "We seem to catch each other at inconvenient times."

"I know you work at la Colombe d'Or, but that's just a job. I hardly know anything else about you."

Pascal looked uncomfortable with the open-ended question, so Mathias rephrased it. "Are you from Montreal originally?"

"Yes," Pascal replied. "I grew up in Mont Royal. I can't imagine living anywhere else. What about you? Where are you from?"

"La Tuque," Mathias said. "I couldn't get out of there fast enough. I couldn't imagine spending my life working in the paper mills, although I do miss the chance to go canoeing every weekend. Not as many places to go when you live in town."

"You like canoeing?" Pascal asked. "I know a couple of places not too far out of town if you ever have a day off. We could leave early and be back in time for dinner." He looked so excited Mathias wanted to lean over and kiss him right then. When his expression suddenly grew more closed and his voice more reserved, Mathias wanted to shake him. "I mean, if you're looking for someone to go with sometime."

The sudden bout of nerves soothed Mathias's own nerves. If Pascal, who had nothing to worry about as far as Mathias was concerned, could be nervous about how Mathias would react, Mathias's own nerves weren't so unreasonable.

"I would love to go canoeing with you sometime. If we make plans in advance, I could even ask for the late shift so we'd have more time."

"What are you doing next weekend?" Pascal blurted out.

"Wishing I were free so I could go canoeing with you," Mathias said. "Unfortunately I have training sessions for the management program at the bank for the next four Saturdays, and I know you spend a lot of Sundays with your parents."

"Not all of them," Pascal said. "I don't want to monopolize all your free time, though. You need time to rest too."

"I can rest when I'm dead," Mathias said with a grin. He leaned closer to Pascal, all but offering him a kiss. "I'd rather spend time with you."

He knew he hadn't misread Pascal's interest, which made the way he suddenly reared back all the more confusing. Mathias frowned and sat back in his seat, focusing on his meal for a moment. The pasta salad was delicious with all the fresh vegetables. "This is really good," he said when Pascal stayed silent.

"Merci," Pascal said. "I don't have a lot of chance to cook. I'm always grabbing a meal at the restaurant between shifts. And when I am home, it's just me, and cooking for one is no fun."

"Why do you think I eat so many frozen dinners?" Mathias said with a smile, trying to draw Pascal out again.

"I guess you have even less time than I do to cook."

"Or even to eat most days," Mathias said. "I've lost ten pounds since I started working at Le Salon."

Pascal raked Mathias with his gaze, his eyes dark with interest. Mathias leaned back in his chair to give Pascal a better view, but the moment he did, Pascal looked away. Mathias frowned at the mixed signals.

Pascal didn't look at him like a man who'd invited a buddy over for lunch, but every time Mathias made any kind of a suggestive move in his direction, Pascal drew back.

It was more than a little confusing.

Whatever Pascal wanted from Mathias, it obviously didn't involve flirting. Mathias could take a hint. No more innuendo. No more suggestive glances. He was more than just an attractive package. He'd find another way of holding Pascal's interest.

"Tell me about the places to go canoeing. I really would love to get back into that."

Pascal relaxed again, affirming Mathias's choice as Pascal began talking about the various lakes scattered north and west, places where they could rent a canoe and spend a few hours away from the city. "Or if you like hiking, there are some great places for that. I used to go all the time with…." For a moment, Mathias thought he'd lost Pascal again, but then he summoned a smile and continued. "With an old friend. I haven't been in fifteen years or more, but I'm sure a lot of those trails are still open, or if not, we could find new ones."

"Hiking sounds great too," Mathias said. "I love running, and the neighborhood is still new enough to me that I see things I missed before, but doing the same routine all the time gets old fast."

"Yeah," Pascal agreed. "The gym is the same way. You said you had training sessions at the bank? What kind of sessions?"

"I'm in a fast-track position," Mathias explained, "that will lead to a middle-management job in a couple of years, but that means that for the next two years or so, I have to work through every department and pretty much every job at the bank. The idea is that I'll understand how it all fits together and what everyone's roles are so I can effectively manage whatever department they decide to put me in when my two years are up. I've been working with customers in a branch with account creation and that sort of thing. The training sessions are to get me ready for the next stage, which will be the credit and collections department. I'm not looking forward to that one. After that, it'll be loans and then investments. I still have a few months before I switch over to the credit and collections department, but this is when the training is being offered, so this is when I have to take it."

"That sounds like quite a commitment," Pascal said.

"It is," Mathias said, "but if you make it through the program, you get quite a commitment from the bank as well in terms of job security and advancement. Once I finish the program and get my first assignment—and maybe even before then, depending on bonuses and how things go—I won't need to keep working at Le Salon. It's a stopgap measure, not a career choice."

Pascal frowned ever so slightly, making Mathias wonder what he had said wrong. "What about you? How long have you been at la Colombe d'Or?"

"Almost twenty years," Pascal said. "I was waiting tables at one of the tourist traps along place Jacques Cartier, making enough to pay the rent on a tiny little apartment when a… a friend told me he'd seen a notice for a position available at la Colombe d'Or. We'd walked by there I don't know how many times, and even through the window I could tell it was a much better restaurant than the place I was working. I figured I didn't have anything to lose, so I put on my best suit and my best smile and applied. They hired me, and I haven't looked back."

"That's great, though," Mathias said. "You so rarely hear of people who manage to stay in a job with that kind of longevity. Average tenure at the bank is something like eight years. It's a little higher at the management level, but while you have a few of the senior executives who have worked their way up through the ranks, most of them were brought in to be executives. They might retire from their current position, but they've got four or five other jobs on their CVs before this one."

"It's a good place to work," Pascal said with a shrug.

"So, if you don't mind my asking, why a restaurant?" Mathias asked. "What made you choose that?"

Pascal shrugged again. "It pays the bills. I don't have any Saturday training sessions to worry about. The only thing I bring home from work is dinner. I get to meet a lot of interesting people, and it's never the same thing twice. There are lot worse ways to earn a living."

"Oh…," Mathias said, Pascal's last comment hitting him like a slap in the face. "Oh, fuck, no, that's not what I meant. God, you must think I'm an insensitive idiot. I didn't mean any of that to sound like a criticism of *your* choices. Oh, fuck, I'm sorry."

Pascal shrugged again. "You're certainly entitled to your opinion."

Mathias wanted to curse again, but that wouldn't help. "I suppose I am, as long as you don't put words in my mouth." He tried to grin and steal one of his father's lines. "It's unsanitary." The joke fell flat, judging by the continued tense set of Pascal's shoulders. "Look, waiting tables at a place like Le Salon isn't the way I want to spend my life, but it's not the way you're spending your life either. I've walked by la Colombe d'Or. I have colleagues who swear they'll never have a business lunch or dinner anywhere else. Working there, it's not the same thing. That *is* a career choice, not just a job to help pay the bills like Le Salon is for me, and I meant what I said about how long you've been there. I bet you practically run the place."

"Not quite," Pascal said. "I don't want the responsibility of keeping up with the books and the orders and dealing with all the personalities, especially in the kitchen. Simon is welcome to keep that. I am the head waiter, though."

"See?" Mathias said. "Upper management."

Pascal smiled at that. "Middle management, anyway," he agreed after a moment. "Simon still deals with the schedules and all that. I just make sure everything runs smoothly on the floor on the days I'm there."

"And on your days off?"

"There are other people there with enough experience to run the floor when I'm not on shift," Pascal said. "I'm good at my job, but it's not the kind of talent that's irreplaceable."

"I don't know," Mathias said with a smile. "I bet you're a lot more irreplaceable than you think. Unless it's seniority alone that determines who the head waiter is."

"Seniority, the patience to deal with the new hires, and the tact to deal with difficult customers," Pascal replied.

"And enough investment in the place to want to do those things," Mathias finished. "See, that's the difference. You *like* what you do. Maybe you even love it, and that's awesome to see. For me, that passion is for the bank. I couldn't do what you do because I don't have the passion for it. That's all I meant when I made the comment about waiting tables. It's not the right choice for me, but it obviously has been the right choice for you."

"Yeah, it is the right choice for me," Pascal said. "And the perks are good too."

"What perks would those be?" Mathias asked. He'd never thought about there being perks in the restaurant business.

"I can take vacation when I want," Pascal said, "as long as there aren't too many people wanting off at the same time. I don't have to wait for a set school vacation or for a project to finish or for it to be convenient to my bosses. I just tell Simon not to put me on the schedule for a couple of weeks, and then I'm free to spend that time however I want. I've taken some amazing trips that I probably wouldn't have been able to do if I'd worked at a different job. Most places would frown at giving me a month off to go to India. Simon just told me to bring back recipe ideas."

"Yeah, I can't imagine asking for a month off," Mathias said. "Certainly not for something like that. I mean, maybe if my parents died and I had to go home to take care of their estate, but even then, I doubt I'd get a month. That's definitely a perk."

"The biggest one, though, is not having work follow me home," Pascal said. "When I take off my apron and walk out that door, I don't have to think about work again until I walk back in again, whether that's twelve hours, two days, or four weeks later."

"And you obviously make enough to live in a place like this and still have money left over for travel and whatever else makes you happy," Mathias said. "I certainly can't say that at the moment. I'm working a second job and still struggling to pay the bills."

"And you're supposed to be the banker with the responsible head on his shoulders," Pascal teased. "Is it really worth it to live here? I mean, when I was your age, I was sharing a flat with two other guys and taking turns sleeping depending on whose shift it was. By the time I got home most nights, my roommate was getting up to leave."

"It's worth it," Mathias said. "Appearance matters in the corporate world, and having the right address, or maybe not having the wrong address, is one of those things people notice."

"You'd know best what's required in your own field," Pascal said, "although it seems like a lot of work for not a lot of payoff."

Mathias grinned. "I wouldn't have met you if I'd gone another route."

"True enough," Pascal said. "You want some more wine?"

"Sure," Mathias said. "You mentioned hiking and canoeing. And of course I know about your books, but what else do you do with your free time?"

"I work," Pascal said. "I work as much as I can while still staying sane for ten months of the year, and then I spend the other two months traveling. Sometimes I'll go a month, like I did to India. Other times, I'll do a week here and a week there."

"Really? I bet you've been to some amazing places!"

"A few," Pascal said. "It's only in the past few years that I've had the freedom and the money to travel as extensively as I wanted."

"Where's your favorite place you've been?"

"That's a hard question. I've liked everywhere I've gone for different reasons." The light in Pascal's eyes as he spoke drew Mathias in. He leaned closer, wanting to hear more.

"Then where did you go last?" Mathias asked.

"Peru," Pascal said. "I went last winter. It was summer there, so it was a nice break from the snow."

"Did you make it up to Machu Picchu?" Mathias asked. "I've always wanted to see it."

"I did," Pascal said. "Do you want to see some pictures?"

"I'd love to!" Mathias said. "I suck at photography, so I'm always envious of people who can take good pictures."

"I'm pretty sure there's nothing more boring than other people's travel photos, but I'll go get my laptop. We can browse through them," Pascal offered. "I haven't gotten around to printing them out and making an album yet. That's the one downside of digital pictures."

"Maybe, but I can think of plenty of upsides. I really would like to see them," Mathias said. He didn't add that it would let him sit closer to Pascal.

"Come inside, then," Pascal said. "As nice as it is outside today, the glare on the laptop screen will make it hard to see the pictures."

Mathias followed Pascal back inside, bringing his dishes with him. He might be a guest, but he wouldn't be a rude one. Pascal thanked him as he put away the pasta salad and went in search of his computer. Mathias took a seat on the couch, figuring it would provide the best option for viewing the pictures and getting a little closer to Pascal.

If the other man would let him, that is. Pascal had blown hot and cold, drawing back at every sign of serious flirting. Interest was fine. Enticement was not. Mathias wondered if he'd misread Pascal's intentions in inviting him for lunch. He'd thought it was a date, but maybe not. Pascal was pretty clearly the only inhabitant of the apartment, but Mathias had seen him more than once with two other men at Le Salon. Could one of them be his lover? The thought pricked his jealousy, but he pushed it down. Meeting up with someone at a bar did not have to mean anything in particular. This was Mathias's problem, not Pascal's, and he refused to let his jealousy ruin a perfectly good relationship before it ever started. He wouldn't be another man's piece on the side, but making a scene now over nothing wouldn't do any good either.

"Do you travel by yourself?" Mathias asked when Pascal came back with his computer.

"I usually go on organized tours," Pascal said, "because they can often get better deals and squeeze more into a trip than I could do on my own, but I take my trips to get away from everyone and everything here.

My friends are great, and I like my colleagues, but sometimes I just need some solitude."

"That makes sense," Mathias said. "Show me your pictures."

They spent the next hour looking through pictures of Peru, and then of France, Italy, and Japan. Mathias sat as close as he could, and Pascal didn't pull away. When it was growing close to time for him to go to work, Mathias leaned closer still, intending to give Pascal a kiss before he left, but Pascal again pulled back.

"Am I misreading things here?" Mathias asked in exasperation. "I was under the impression this was a date."

"It is," Pascal said.

"Then why do you keep pulling away from me?" Mathias asked.

"Because I'm not interested in a fling," Pascal replied.

Mathias frowned. "I wasn't aware I was offering one. A kiss doesn't have to mean anything more than just that. It doesn't have to be a prelude to sex."

"I know," Pascal said, "but I didn't want to lead you on."

"So instead you're going to run me off?" Mathias said. "For what it's worth, I like you. I enjoyed our date. I'd like to see you again, but I don't want to feel like you're going to freak out on me every time I touch you or flirt with you."

"Sorry," Pascal said. "It's been a while since I've done this."

"Had a date? I find that hard to believe."

"Had a date I wanted to mean something."

"Then you're not opposed to flings in general, just to one with me?" Mathias teased, but the words held no heat, not when Pascal's comment meant Mathias was different than anyone he'd been seeing recently. Pascal was old enough that Mathias didn't delude himself into thinking he was Pascal's first serious relationship, but he was more than willing to be Pascal's next serious one if that was what Pascal wanted.

"I'm not twenty anymore," Pascal said. "I'm not built for messing around. It was okay when I was younger, but that was a long time ago."

"You're not as old as all that," Mathias insisted.

"I turned forty-eight in April," Pascal said. "I'm not as young as all that either."

Mathias smiled, and when he leaned forward to kiss Pascal this time, Pascal didn't pull away. Mathias didn't linger, as much as he wanted to.

He'd settle for a swift buss of lips this time in exchange for more—and better—in the future. "I have a thing for men in their prime," Mathias admitted when he'd sat back. "And you're the perfect example."

"I'm almost afraid to ask, but how old are you?"

"Twenty-four," Mathias said. "I'll be twenty-five in December. I'm not jailbait."

"No, just half my age," Pascal said.

Mathias squeezed his hand. He wanted to kiss Pascal again, but he'd already been that forward once. He didn't want to push his luck. "Only for another few months. Then it'll be less than half."

Pascal laughed as Mathias had wanted him to. "Okay, you win." He looked at the clock. "When do you need to leave?"

"In a few minutes," Mathias said. "Come by the bar tonight?"

"I have to work too," Pascal reminded him. "I'm off on Wednesday. I could come by then."

"Please do. And I'll text you once I know what my schedule is for the workshops, and we'll plan another lunch or something."

"I'm looking forward to it already."

CHAPTER 7

PASCAL'S PHONE rang at precisely three o'clock the next afternoon. "How was it?"

"Hello to you too, René," Pascal said with a roll of his eyes, even knowing René couldn't see him. "It was... good."

"You don't sound convinced," René said.

"No, it was," Pascal said, thinking back over his date with Mathias, as if he'd thought of much else since then. "A few rocky patches, but it was a first date. There are always a few rocky patches."

"Are you seeing him again?"

"We live in the same building. I'm quite sure we'll see each other whether we want to or not."

"That's not what I meant, and you know it," René said. "Do you have another date?"

"We have a date to make a date," Pascal replied.

"What's that supposed to mean?"

"It means I'm going by the bar on Wednesday to see him, and he's going to text me once he gets his work schedule for the next few weeks so we can find a time we're both free to do something," Pascal said. "What did you think it meant?"

"With you, who knows?" René retorted. "So you've gotten over all that crap about being too old for him?"

"No, but I told him how old I am, and it didn't bother him, so I'm trying not to let it bother me," Pascal said. "I know how it must seem, but I really am trying. I've been alone for a long time. I'm ready not to be alone anymore."

"You know Benjamin and I will support you whatever you decide, *n'est-ce pas*? We may give you a hard time occasionally, but we want what's best for you."

"You just think you know what that is, even when you don't," Pascal said.

"Or even when you don't," René replied. "I know, it's easy for us to say that. We've never stood by helplessly while the man we expected to spend our lives with wasted away and died. We've never stood at his grave and wondered where everything went wrong. You're absolutely right about that. We haven't, and I'll thank every god in the pantheon for that, but that doesn't mean we haven't seen you hurting and lonely, drifting from unsatisfactory date to unsatisfactory date because you were looking for a replacement for Robert or because you weren't ready to commit to the success of a new relationship. This kid is different. I can see that even after just seeing him at the bar a few times. Maybe he's what you need, maybe he isn't, but I don't want to see you lose him because you aren't willing to take the chance."

"We kissed," Pascal said. "Well, he kissed me. I was so surprised I can't say I exactly kissed him back."

"Idiot," René said, but his voice betrayed his affection. "Why didn't you kiss him back?"

"I've been so careful since Robert died not to lead anyone on, not to hint in any way at more than I'm willing to give," Pascal said. "I've forgotten how to send any other kind of signal."

"I know you've had sex since he died."

That depended on how he defined sex, but Pascal wasn't getting into *that* conversation with René. Besides, that wasn't the point. "That's sex. I'm talking about an actual relationship. There *is* a difference."

"I know there is," René said, "but one doesn't preclude the other. Did you tell him any of this?"

"Just that I didn't want a fling," Pascal said.

"I'm not saying you need to tell him your whole life story the next time you have a date," René said, "but if this is going anywhere, he needs to understand what you've gone through and where your soft spots are. Even accidental bumps can hurt beyond repair. If he knows where they are, he won't hit them by mistake."

"I know." Pascal dreaded having to tell Mathias about Robert. René and Benjamin had lived through that time with him. They knew without words when an anniversary, bittersweet or bad, approached. They understood when he needed time to himself around those dark days, when he needed to get away for however long it took him to be ready to face the world again. Having to explain all that to someone else would be excruciating. "I just have to find the right time to do it. If things aren't going to work out, if he's not going to stick around, there's no reason to put myself through that."

René didn't answer right away, but when he did and changed the subject, Pascal knew he'd accepted Pascal's assertion. "If you didn't have sex, what did you do?"

"We had lunch, we talked about his job at the bank, about working at la Colombe d'Or, and then we ended up looking at travel pictures," Pascal said.

"You made him look at your pictures?" René said. "Lame, buddy. Really lame."

"He asked," Pascal said. "I mentioned that I traveled when I could, and he asked where I'd gone. When I told him, he said he'd love to see my pictures. And since that's when he kissed me, you can't complain too much because if we'd spent the whole time sitting on the balcony, he couldn't have gotten close enough for a kiss."

"Whatever works, I guess," René replied philosophically. "When are you seeing him again?"

"Wednesday night at the bar," Pascal said. "It's my night off, but he has to work, so I'm going to drop by and see him."

"Adrien's going to love you, with all the extra money you're spending there these days," René teased.

"As long as I don't distract his employees," Pascal replied. "I don't want Mathias to get in trouble again because of me."

"Pathetic." The tone of René's voice was one usually reserved for cute puppies and chubby-cheeked babies. Pascal shook his head, but he couldn't help the smile it brought to his face.

"YOU LOOK like the cat that ate the canary," Louis said when Mathias arrived at work on Monday. "Good weekend?"

"Pretty good," Mathias said.

"Then what's with the grin?" Louis asked. "Did you get laid?"

"No," Mathias said. "It's not like that."

"You had a date, right? With the cute panther in your building."

"He's not a panther," Mathias protested.

"He's over forty, and he's dating a much younger guy. That looks like a panther to me," Louis said.

"Yeah, but that makes it sound like there's something perverted about it, and it's really not like that. We had lunch. We talked. We looked at photos he's taken on different trips," Mathias said. "We talked about books. Did you know he's friends with Martine Caron? He gave me her e-mail so I can tell her how much I like her books!"

"Her e-mail is in the books," Louis pointed out. "At least in the more recent ones."

"Yeah, but he has signed copies of all her books, not just the Pascal St-Laurent ones. He knows her from the restaurant."

"Okay, that is pretty cool. Did you totally geek out on him?"

"Yeah, a little," Mathias admitted, "but he didn't mind. I got the feeling he liked it when I stopped trying to be suave and sophisticated and was just myself."

"But that's a good thing," Louis said. "Not to say you aren't suave and sophisticated, but you need a place you can let go of everything and just relax. And if this is going where you want it to, you need that place to be with him."

"He also said he wasn't looking for a fling," Mathis said. "So that's promising, but he's… well, he's everything I'm not, Louis, and I'm still not entirely sure what he sees in me or why he'd want to be with me beyond something fun and flirty. He doesn't talk about it, but there are shadows in his eyes sometimes, like he's been hurt in the past and hasn't gotten over it."

"And yet he doesn't want a fling," Louis said. "So either it was a fling that hurt him, or he's ready to try for something serious again despite whatever hurt was in the past."

"I'm not sure I'm strong enough to be someone's rehabilitation," Mathias replied.

"Has he asked you to be?"

"Well, no."

"Then you're projecting thoughts and emotions onto him," Louis said. "You met up, had lunch, talked about books and work and travel. That doesn't sound like rehabilitation. It sounds like two guys getting to know each other better. And *that* sounds like the beginning of a relationship."

"You think I should go for it?"

"I think you shouldn't give up just because it's not the most obvious or straightforward thing you've ever done," Louis said. "You aren't one to take the easy road. If you were, you wouldn't have picked the management track. You wouldn't be living where you do and working a second job to pay for it. You'd be in La Tuque working in a paper mill or as a canoe guide. Isn't that what you told me most of your high school classmates were doing with their lives?"

"Pretty much," Mathias said. "I mean, a few of them will get jobs in the local infrastructure. La Tuque needs teachers and city employees and that kind of thing, but the growth is low, so there's only a few spots available each year."

"Still, you didn't pick that way either," Louis said. "Do the same with your personal life. If he's worth taking an interest in, he's worth dealing with the bumps in the road."

Mathias nodded. He agreed with Louis mostly. He wasn't concerned about the amount of work a relationship with Pascal would require from him. He was worried Pascal would get fed up with the differences between them. Mathias couldn't afford to travel with Pascal, even if he could take the time off to do it, but Pascal obviously loved it too much to want to give it up. He needed someone who had the money and flexibility to go with him, not someone who probably wouldn't be going anywhere but home to La Tuque for family occasions for at least the next few years.

He could enjoy it while it lasted, though, and maybe get enough experience out of it not to feel so green the next time he met someone who caught his eye.

BY THE time Pascal got all his errands run, all his shopping done, his laundry in the wash, and his apartment tidied up, it was already dinnertime, he hadn't been to the gym, and he was exhausted.

Will you be terribly disappointed if I don't come to the bar tonight? He texted to Mathias. *I'm worn out and I haven't had dinner yet.*

Join me at Café Champlain for dinner. It'll be rushed, but at least I'll get to see you, Mathias texted back a moment later.

Pascal should have said no, but the idea that Mathias had looked forward to seeing him was enough to get Pascal off the couch and into a nicer shirt than the T-shirt he'd worn all day.

When?

Now. I'll wait for you downstairs.

I'll be right down.

Pascal checked to make sure he had his wallet and hurried down to meet Mathias for dinner. As expected, Mathias was dressed for his shift at the bar: spiky hair, skintight jeans, painted-on T-shirt. He looked positively sinful.

"Hi," Mathias said when Pascal met him on the doorstep. He leaned in and kissed Pascal's cheek. "Thank you for indulging me."

"I'm pretty sure everyone at Café Champlain is going to think you're indulging me," Pascal said. "You look good enough to eat."

Mathias flashed a cheeky grin. "They'll think I'm lucky to have snagged such a handsome sugar daddy."

"I'm no sugar daddy," Pascal said as they walked down the street to the café. "I don't make enough for that. And don't put yourself down that way."

"You look good enough for it," Mathias said, "and they can think what they want about me. I know and you know it's not like that. Who cares what they think? It's like the patrons at the bar. If they think there's a chance I might actually be interested in them, they'll tip better. They don't need to know I put all the numbers they give me in the trash at the end of the night."

"You didn't put mine in the trash," Pascal said.

"You aren't just a patron at the bar," Mathias replied. "I… um… I e-mailed Martine Caron today on my lunch break. I told her you'd given me her e-mail because I was such a big fan. I hope you don't mind."

"Of course not." Pascal didn't mind, per se, but he was sure to hear about it when his ladies came to the restaurant again in a couple of weeks.

They reached the café and ordered quickly. "I have training all day on Saturday and 'homework' that I'll have to do on Sunday this weekend," Mathias said as they waited for their food. "But I'm off on Tuesday next week. If you're not working, I thought we could have a nice dinner."

"Unfortunately, I am," Pascal said. "I can try to switch, but I'm not sure anyone will be able to. What about the Saturday after?"

"I've got four weekends of this crap," Mathias said. "I keep telling myself it'll be worth it."

"That's right. You told me. What's the training on this time?" Pascal asked.

"Asset management in the credit department," Mathias said. "It's not the area I want to pursue, but part of this track I'm on is a two- to four-month stint in every department."

"Once that's done, will you have some say about what area you work in?"

"Well, I still have to apply within the departments, and they have to need someone, but I'll have a lot better chance of getting what I want than if I hadn't done the program."

"Then it'll be worth it," Pascal agreed. "You just have to stay focused on the goal."

"That's what Louis keeps telling me. He's my mentor in the program. He finished a couple of years ago and is helping me out now," Mathias said. "He's become a good friend, as well."

The waiter forestalled Pascal's reply with their food. Pascal figured that was fortunate since his immediate reaction was jealousy, an emotion he didn't have any right to express just yet.

"Do you have your schedule at Le Salon for the week after next yet?" Pascal asked as they started eating.

"I'll get it tonight. Why?"

"Because I have to put in my requests, if I have any, for that week tomorrow. If I know what night you're off, I can request it, and we can have a proper dinner date. If you'd like to, that is."

"I'd love to," Mathias said. "I was trying to figure out how to get through four weeks without seeing you for more than a few minutes at a time."

"Text me when you get your schedule," Pascal said. "I'll put my request in first thing tomorrow morning."

"What are you going to do with your night off?" Mathias asked.

"Honestly?" Pascal said. Mathias nodded. "Read Hélène's latest book and go to sleep early. I'm not sure why I'm so tired tonight, but I'm not going to stay up late."

"Lucky you," Mathias said with a grin. "I'll be at the bar until one and at work at eight in the morning."

Pascal didn't ask Mathias how long he could keep up that kind of schedule. Mathias was young, and Pascal remembered having more reserves of energy at that age than he had now. "We'll have dinner in two weeks, and we'll spend a day canoeing as soon as your training course ends. How does that sound?"

"Amazing," Mathias said as he finished his meal. "I hate to eat and run, but I don't want to be late." He pulled some money out of his wallet. "This'll cover my meal. Do you mind waiting for the check?"

"No, go," Pascal said, "but when we go out in two weeks, it's my treat."

Mathias smiled. "Okay, but I get to pick the restaurant, then. And next time, we'll switch."

Pascal thought it should be the other way around, but he didn't say anything. If Mathias wanted to pick the restaurant, Pascal would let him. He could afford dinner at wherever Mathias chose, and he could make sure to choose somewhere interesting but inexpensive when it was Mathias's turn to pay.

CHAPTER 8

PASCAL KNEW the minute he approached the table that his ladies had something up their collective sleeve. Camille's smile was just a touch broader than usual, and Martine gave him a knowing look that spoke volumes about their plans. Well, about the existence of their plans anyway.

"Bonsoir, mesdames," he said with the most genuine smile he'd given anyone all night. The fact that genuine with them meant a smirk that would probably get him fired with anyone else was irrelevant. They teased him as hard as he teased them. "A round of cosmos as usual?"

"What else would we drink?" Hélène asked with a light laugh. "Unless you've got something new to suggest."

Pascal had a brief flash of Mathias offering him the pear martini. "Actually, I might," he said slowly. "I'm not sure we have everything we need to make it, though. I'll check with the bar. If you don't like it, the round is on me."

"Really?" Martine teased. "A new friend and now a new drink? You're full of surprises tonight, Pascal!"

He just smiled. They wouldn't let it go at that, but he could delay the inquisition by a few minutes at least.

Nick at the bar had everything for a pear martini and even had an idea of the right proportions of the different ingredients. He gave Pascal a taste before he poured the glasses for the customers, and it tasted very much like what Mathias had served him.

"Here we are," Pascal said as he returned to the table. "Who's going to do the honors?"

Hélène picked up the glass he set in front of her and took a sip. "Very nice," she said. "I'm not sure anything will ever replace cosmos with you, but this is a nice change."

"Good," Pascal said. "I'm glad you like them. A friend is trying to get me to branch out, and this one was a success."

"Tell us about this friend," Martine said. "Is it the same young man who sent me such a nice e-mail last week?"

Pascal knew how this game worked. It had been a while since they'd last played it, but he hadn't forgotten how. "I would imagine you receive quite a few e-mails each week."

"But not that mention you as the way the person got my e-mail. If the icon on his e-mail is what he looks like, he's quite the looker," Martine teased.

"I haven't seen his e-mail icon," Pascal replied smoothly.

Martine gave an exasperated laugh. "Fine," she said. "His name is Mathias Perras. Who is he?"

"Who is he to you?" Hélène specified. "And more importantly, why are you so hesitant to talk about him?"

"He's...." Pascal sighed, not sure how to reply. "It's complicated. Do you want any appetizers?"

"The best things always are," Nicole said. "I'll have the French onion soup."

Hélène, Camille, and Martine ordered as well, and Pascal beat a swift retreat to put their order in and check on his other tables, but also to regroup and try to decide how to answer them. He already knew they wouldn't be satisfied with less.

Wednesdays were not usually a busy night at la Colombe d'Or, a fact Pascal normally appreciated when his ladies came in, but tonight it took away his excuses for not coming back to check on them—and field their questions.

"The appetizers should be out in a minute," he said. "Have you decided on dinner?"

"I'm sorry, Pascal," Martine said. "I shouldn't have pushed when you clearly didn't want to talk about it. Don't go all cold and professional on us. I won't say anything else about it."

"I'm just not sure what to say," Pascal said. "He lives in my building and works nights at the bar I like. He works days at a bank, and yeah, it's complicated."

"It sounds like the good kind of complicated to me," Nicole said, "but Martine's right. We won't push. I'll have the chateaubriand, please, medium rare."

"The poisson meunière," Hélène said.

"The cailles en brochettes for me," Camille said.

"And I'll have the rôti de porc," Martine said.

Pascal took their orders back to the kitchen and checked on his other tables. He only had two others tonight and probably wouldn't have more unless the restaurant got unusually busy. Simon was used to Pascal's ladies visiting and did his best not to overload Pascal when they were in so he could visit with them as well as wait on their table.

His other tables tonight were business dinners, from what he could tell, and so would probably appreciate less obtrusive service anyway. He took appetizers to one table and entrées to another before he returned to check on his ladies. "Another round?" he asked. "Or cosmos this time?"

"Cosmo," Hélène said.

"I'll have another of these," Camille said.

"Cosmo."

"One of these."

"However much I like him—and I do, probably more than I should—nothing can come of it. Not really. We're too different," Pascal blurted out. "I'll get your drinks."

By the time the drinks were ready, their appetizers were too, and he had his hands full for a few minutes getting everything served.

"Sometimes differences are good things," Hélène said after all the dishes were in the appropriate places. "It makes life interesting."

"It makes your books interesting," Pascal said. "It makes life hard."

"It can make life hard," Nicole agreed, and Pascal remembered the pictures she'd shown him of her husband and family. He was Asian. She was not. And the clash of the two cultures had caused more than one disagreement. He'd overheard a rant or few over the years. "It can also be incredibly enriching. Maybe it isn't worth it. But maybe it is. Don't give up just because it's hard."

Right now it wasn't hard, but Pascal could see all the ways it could become that way. "I won't," he said, "but he has to do the same."

"YOU WORE blue," Mathias said when Pascal opened the door. He'd texted Pascal on the train ride home from the bank, a habit he'd gotten into over the past two weeks since their lunch date. He might not be able to see Pascal every day, but he was determined to stay in touch and keep himself in Pascal's thoughts by sharing what pieces he could of his day.

"You asked me to," Pascal said with that little smile Mathias already loved coaxing out of him.

"It brings out your eyes," Mathias said, just as he had in the text he'd sent earlier.

"You should just be glad I still had this shirt. I haven't worn blue in… a long time."

Mathias could hear a story in those words, but it didn't take more than a glance at Pascal's face to stop him from asking for it. Whatever— or whoever—had convinced him to stop wearing blue, it had left an indelible mark. That thought made the butterflies start in Mathias's belly again. Pascal had worn blue at his request despite whatever had stopped him from doing so recently.

"Are you ready?" Mathias asked. "I thought we'd take a cab. The restaurant isn't easy to get to on the bus."

"We can do that," Pascal said, "or we can take my car. I regularly consider getting rid of it since I don't use it very often, but then there's something like tonight, and I'm glad I have it."

Mathias wished he had the luxury of keeping a car, but it just wasn't feasible on his current salary or in his current situation. "If you want to drive, that's fine, but if we take a cab, you don't have to worry about driving home."

"Are you planning on getting me drunk?" Pascal asked slyly.

Mathias stepped a little closer. "Will I get past first base if I do?"

"No, you have to buy me dinner for that," Pascal quipped back.

Mathias whipped out his phone. "When's your next night off?"

Pascal laughed, and Mathias relaxed as he put his phone back. The tension that had invested Pascal every time Mathias had flirted when they'd had lunch didn't make an appearance this time. He was making progress.

"Where are we going?" Pascal asked.

"La Petite Ardoise." Mathias hoped Pascal would approve of his choice. He'd tried to pick somewhere nice without being expensive. "It has an outdoor terrace so we can sit there and enjoy the beautiful weather. My parents took me there for dinner when I got the job at the bank. It was very good, not too pricey, and a good ambiance."

"You don't have to sell me on your choice," Pascal said. "I told you to choose a restaurant. Whatever you chose is fine."

LA PETITE Ardoise was everything Mathias had said it would be, the dark wood around the windows and holding the flower boxes giving the restaurant a rustic charm. The red-brick walls and patio of the interior courtyard only added to the warm feeling, and the chalkboard with the day's specials topped it off perfectly. Combine that with the genuine side Mathias had been displaying since he arrived home, the sweet, funny guy Pascal had gotten to know through their texted conversations over the past two weeks, and Pascal was pretty sure it was the recipe for a perfect evening.

Pascal always enjoyed reading the menus at other restaurants. La Colombe d'Or was known for its upscale, trendy menu, but it meant that often the mainstays of traditional French cuisine weren't on the menu because they were too "basic" to qualify. La Petite Ardoise included galettes, crêpes, and simple dishes like steak-frites along with their lobster tail special and filet mignon. Pascal was looking forward to the simple meal. "What are you getting?" he asked Mathias.

"I was thinking about maybe a galette," Mathias said. "I haven't had one in a while, and they're always good."

"So maybe a bottle of rosé?" Pascal suggested. "Or would you rather a white wine?"

"You're the wine expert," Mathias insisted. "You tell me which one would go best."

Pascal smiled a little at Mathias's eagerness to please. "It's not just about what 'goes well.' It's also about what the people drinking it like. No matter how perfect someone else thinks a wine pairing is, if you don't like the wine to begin with, you aren't going to enjoy the pairing."

"I get that," Mathias said, "but you're assuming I know what I like, and I don't. At least if we get a wine that pairs well with the food, we won't have to worry about me not liking it because it's a bad pairing."

"You liked the rosé we had with lunch," Pascal said, "and this one is similar, so let's go with that one."

He placed their drink order when their server returned and then gestured for Mathias to order. He ordered the salade niçoise and turned his attention back to Mathias.

"I've been thinking about canoeing," he said. "I know you have two more weeks of training before you're free on a Saturday, but do you want to try to do something the Saturday after that? It'll only be September. It won't be too cold to spend a day on the water. Le Parc de la Rivière-des-Mille-Îles is outside of Laval. We could go there for a few hours without it eating too much time out of our Saturday."

"That sounds wonderful," Mathias said. "I haven't been canoeing since last summer, and I really miss it."

Pascal smiled contentedly. He liked the idea of making Mathias happy.

BY THE time they got back to their apartment building later in the evening, Pascal had given up trying to figure out what had given him a buzz—the wine or the constant expression of delight on Mathias's face as the evening had gone on. They hadn't had any missteps like on their first date, neither of them saying anything to trigger bad moments in the other. Even wearing the blue shirt, the only one he still had after Robert died, hadn't been enough to bring Pascal down from the high of being out with the most attractive man in the restaurant. He might not understand *why* Mathias wanted to be with him, but he couldn't argue *that* Mathias wanted to be with him.

He walked Mathias back to his apartment. He didn't want the date to end, but he also didn't want to pressure Mathias in any way. He'd been too insistent on their first date about taking things slowly to be anything other than a gentleman now.

Mathias opened the door and turned to smile at Pascal. "I don't have much in the way of wine, but I can offer you a beer."

"You don't have to offer me anything," Pascal reminded him.

"What if I want to offer you something?" Mathias replied as he took a step back, creating space for Pascal to enter the small apartment.

Pascal took a stuttering breath at all the ways he could read that statement. He couldn't throw all his good intentions out the window simply because Mathias was looking at him like *that*. He couldn't! Mathias slipped his hand into Pascal's and tugged. Pascal gave up resisting and allowed Mathias to lead him inside.

Mathias's apartment was about half the size of Pascal's, much as Pascal had expected. He'd lived in one of the units on this floor when he'd first moved into the building, so the postage-stamp living room was no surprise. Then Mathias stepped close, pulling Pascal down and into a kiss, and Pascal forgot about the size of the living room and anything else other than returning the kiss. Mathias's lips were slightly rough, a little chapped, not surprising since he had a habit of biting his bottom lip. Pascal had watched him doing it more than once over the course of dinner. Mathias kissed with the same eager enthusiasm he'd displayed all night, leaning into Pascal and licking at his lips the same way he licked at his own.

Pascal deepened the kiss, stroking his tongue over the seam of Mathias's lips until they parted and he could delve inside. He could taste the coffee they'd had after dinner on Mathias's tongue, the dark scent mingling with the lingering hint of cologne. He slid his hands around Mathias's waist to pull him closer. Even through Mathias's shirt—his jacket lay discarded on the floor where Mathias had dropped it when he moved in to start this kiss—Pascal could feel the heat emanating from Mathias's skin.

A part of him wanted to strip the cloth away. It had been so long since he had touched and been touched, since he'd been able to find that connection with another person. Robert had made him promise not to mourn forever after he died, but Pascal had never felt completely right letting him go. Now, with Mathias in his arms, pressed against him, warmth radiating through Pascal, some of that old grief eased, and Pascal ached for more.

He could have more. That much was obvious from Mathias's body language. If Pascal started undressing him, if he started walking Mathias toward the bedroom, Mathias wouldn't stop him. He'd probably egg him on the whole time.

That thought gave Pascal the strength to break the kiss and rest his forehead against Mathias's. Mathias leaned in and stole another soft kiss, which Pascal returned before drawing back. He stroked the smooth line of Mathias's jaw with his thumb, feeling the slightest hint of whiskers beneath the soft skin. "I'm not taking you to bed tonight," he said, his voice tender despite the words.

"I know," Mathias said. "You could take me to the couch, though."

"You could stop trying to seduce me," Pascal replied with a smile and another swift kiss.

"Why would I do that?" Mathias asked. "We've had a wonderful evening. I'm buzzed. You're ridiculously attractive, and you're in my apartment."

"We did have a wonderful evening," Pascal said, "and I'm looking forward to many more wonderful evenings."

"Then why shouldn't I try to seduce you?" Mathias asked, his voice still pitched low and sultry.

"Because you're worth more than sex," Pascal replied seriously. "When we finally go to bed, I want it to mean something. We're getting there, but if I take you to bed right now, you'll always wonder if it was just about the sex, if I'm with you because I want to tap your hot ass."

Mathias smirked at him as he slid a hand between their bodies and rubbed over Pascal's crotch. Pascal bucked into the touch even as he told himself to pull away. "You do want to tap it."

"I never said I didn't," Pascal said, "but that's not all I want, and it's not even primarily what I want."

"What do you want?" Mathias asked as he drew Pascal toward the couch.

Pascal waited until they had settled on the thin cushions. "Everything."

"How is sex not part of everything?" Mathias asked.

"I was in my twenties by the time anyone really began to understand what HIV was, how it was transmitted, or how terrible a disease it really was," Pascal said. "It's a miracle, honestly, that I'm not infected. I can't tell you how many people I lost in those years as the reality of the disease and what it meant to the community became more and more obvious. Those experiences changed the way I see things, especially where sex is concerned. Sex *is* part of everything, but for me, it's the last part. The icing on the cake, so to speak, not the sum total of the dessert."

"I can understand that," Mathias said. "So how do you see this working?"

"I don't know exactly," Pascal admitted. "I haven't done this in a long time. Tonight has been amazing. Dinner was fantastic—the restaurant was an inspired choice. Getting to sit and talk to you was even better. And kissing you… well, you know how I feel about that. So I guess the answer is to do more of the same until the right moment."

"And what makes the right moment?"

"We'll know it when it happens," Pascal replied. "That's all I can say."

CHAPTER 9

"TOMORROW CAN'T come soon enough," Mathias said as he sat with Louis on Friday two weeks later. "I'm finally done with the credit department training, and I get to see Pascal again."

"I thought you were trying to see each other on your respective nights off."

"Trying, yes," Mathias said, "but we managed dinner two weeks ago, and I've barely seen him since. He came by the bar one night while I was working, but that's not the same thing. I can flirt with him a bit when I check on his table, but it's not the same. He's not the same. He doesn't respond to the flirting at the bar the way he does when I flirt with him elsewhere."

"Have you asked him about that?" Louis asked.

"Not something to really ask in a text," Mathias said, "and we haven't had a chance to talk except in passing otherwise."

"What are you doing tomorrow?" Louis asked.

"Going canoeing," Mathias said. "I haven't been since last summer. Too cold over the winter and no time since I moved here. I've missed it."

"Was this his idea or yours?" Louis asked.

"His," Mathias said. "He mentioned it when we went out to dinner. He found a place near here where we could go and get back in time for me to work my shift tomorrow night. Why?"

"Because it's something you obviously want to do, so if he suggested it, that's a good sign," Louis said. "He isn't just looking for a pretty twink to show off."

"He's not," Mathias said, feeling incredibly defensive on Pascal's behalf. They'd only kissed a few times. Pascal hadn't even groped him when he came in after their last date. Of course Mathias hoped maybe the canoeing trip would end with more kisses and hopefully some groping, but Pascal certainly wasn't the one driving that side of their relationship. Whatever concerns Mathias might have about their relationship, the thought that Pascal was just looking for a boy toy to show off was not one of them.

MATHIAS WAS glad Pascal had offered to drive them to Laval the next day because he was in no shape to drive or negotiate public transportation. He'd gotten home around three in the morning and with the hour drive to Laval and wanting to have enough time to enjoy their trip before they had to drive back to Montréal, they had decided to meet at eight. Four and a half hours' sleep was not enough, as far as Mathias was concerned. He managed to brush his teeth and get dressed before Pascal knocked on the door, but not much more.

"Coffee," Pascal said, handing Mathias a Tim Hortons cup. "I thought you might need it."

Mathias took a sip of the invigorating ambrosia and leaned in for a kiss. Pascal gave him a quick one, only lingering long enough to tease Mathias with a swipe of his tongue across Mathias's lips. "Bastard," Mathias muttered.

"We don't have to go if you aren't feeling up to it," Pascal offered. "You can go back to sleep, and we can get lunch or something this afternoon."

"Are you coming to bed with me?" Mathias asked.

"You wouldn't get any sleep if I did."

Desire flashed hot and fast through Mathias at the provocative words. "Promise?"

Pascal crowded into his space, so close Mathias could feel the waves of lust crashing through him. The kiss that followed was anything but quick as Pascal invaded Mathias's mouth, languidly claiming every inch with a self-possession that drove Mathias wild. *This* was what he loved about older men: the confidence that came with enough experience to know what they were doing and to do it with conviction. He threw himself into the kiss with enthusiasm, sucking on Pascal's tongue and tangling his own around it. Pascal backed him against the wall and pinned him there as the kiss continued, and Mathias knew he'd give Pascal whatever he wanted. If Pascal gave the slightest indication, Mathias would strip right there or drop to his knees and strip Pascal.

"You're going to be the death of me," Pascal muttered as he broke the kiss and took a step back. "We're going canoeing, not to bed."

"You're the one who brought it up." Mathias could hear the tremble in his voice, and the darkening of Pascal's eyes indicated he'd heard it too. For a moment Mathias thought he'd broken through Pascal's reserve and would get what he'd wanted since the moment he'd laid eyes on Pascal, but Pascal just kissed him again swiftly and left it at that.

"If we're going canoeing, we should go. If you need to sleep, I'll leave so you can."

"I won't fall back asleep," Mathias said. "Once I'm awake, that's pretty much it. I'll sleep in tomorrow."

"You'll be exhausted tonight."

"I'll be exhausted tonight anyway," Mathias insisted. "I want to spend the day with you."

To his relief, Pascal didn't argue anymore.

DESPITE HIS insistence he wouldn't fall back asleep, Mathias dozed in the car on the way to Laval, but once they were out of the car and moving around in the crisp September air, he felt his energy returning. The coffee in his cup had long since grown cold, so he tossed it and accepted another cup from the gear shack at the canoe rental place. Pascal took a cup as well while they waited for the guides to prepare their equipment.

"How long has it been since you last went canoeing?" Mathias asked.

"A few years," Pascal replied, "but it's not something you forget once you've learned how to do it."

"I wasn't worried about that," Mathias said quickly. "I was just curious. There's still so much I don't know about you."

"Sorry," Pascal said. "There are things I don't like to remember, much less talk about."

"So talk about things you do like to remember," Mathias prompted. "Surely not all the memories are bad ones."

"No, they're not," Pascal replied. "But even the good ones are so tied up in the bad ones that it's hard to separate them sometimes."

Mathias tried to imagine what might have happened to leave Pascal with those kinds of memories. He didn't come up with anything good. "Do you want me not to ask? I don't want to make you think about bad stuff."

"No," Pascal said. "I may not answer you, but that shouldn't stop you from asking. I have dark places in my past, times I don't want to go back to, but that's my problem, not yours."

"My mother always says a trouble shared is a trouble halved. I know I'm young and don't have a lot of experience, but… well, if you ever want to talk about it, I'll listen."

"Thank you," Pascal said. "The offer means a lot, even if I never take you up on it."

Mathias hoped Pascal would take him up on it eventually. If he didn't, Mathias would worry constantly about bumping those dark places unintentionally and causing problems between them. He let it go for now, though, because this wasn't the time or the place to push. "Do you want bow or stern?"

Pascal grinned, the expression on his face turning intent again as he raked his gaze over Mathias. "There are advantages to both, but I usually go for stern."

Mathias swallowed hard, trying to wet his suddenly dry mouth. Pascal's words were simple enough, but the way he looked at Mathias added significance to them. He felt his ass clench in anticipation.

The day had suddenly become a lot more interesting.

"DO WE have to go back?" Mathias asked as they paused near the riverbank two hours later. "Can't we just stay out here on the river?"

"Adrien might not appreciate that," Pascal said. "For that matter, Simon at la Colombe d'Or probably wouldn't appreciate it either. I'm opening tonight, so I have to be at the restaurant at four."

"We need a weekend off," Mathias decided. "Two full days where neither of us has to work or visit family or do anything other than just spend time together."

"As lovely as that sounds," Pascal said—and it sounded lovely!—"I'm not sure how realistic it is, not without a reason to give our respective bosses. Especially for you. I've been at la Colombe d'Or long enough I could probably just tell Simon that I need a weekend off, but Adrien doesn't know you that well or have that kind of loyalty to you yet."

"Yeah, cute twinks are a dime a dozen on rue Sainte-Catherine," Mathias agreed with a sigh. "And that's all I am to him."

"To him," Pascal agreed, "but only to him. You're certainly more than that to me."

Mathias swiveled in the seat of the canoe so he could look back at Pascal. The intensity in his brown eyes took him aback. With Mathias facing away from him all morning as they canoed, Pascal had found himself talking more than he had in years, lulled into a sense of safety because he couldn't see Mathias's face. All of that was gone now that Mathias was looking his way again.

"What am I to you?" Mathias asked breathlessly.

"I don't know yet," Pascal replied honestly. "It's too soon to say for sure, but we talk all the time. I like spending time with you. You make me laugh and get me out of my usual routine and…." He took a deep breath. "I still haven't figured out exactly what you see in me, but when I look at you, I see my second chance."

"Maybe we should go back to Montréal now," Mathias said huskily.

Pascal was tempted, *so* tempted by the offer, but he wasn't quite ready. "We can go back," he said, "but there are some things I need to tell you first. If you still want this after that, we'll talk about it."

"You sound like you expect me to go running for the hills," Mathias said.

"You wouldn't be the first if you did," Pascal replied, "and I wouldn't blame you any more than I did them."

"And if I don't?" Mathias asked.

If he didn't, Pascal was pretty sure he'd just lay his heart at Mathias's feet and be done with it.

BY THE time they got off the river, dropped their canoes at the rental place, and made the drive back to Montréal, it was nearly two thirty, late enough that Mathias had to go immediately to get ready for the bar.

"We'll see each other next Saturday," Mathias promised as Pascal parked the car. "And you can come into the bar on Tuesday when you're off work. It's not the same as us getting time alone to talk, but at least we can see each other. It'll give us something to look forward to."

Pascal wouldn't have used those words in connection with the conversation he knew he needed to have with Mathias. He needed to explain about Robert, about his past and everything, but they didn't have time now, so it would have to wait. "I'll see you on Tuesday," Pascal promised. "Even if I just come in for a few minutes."

They reached Mathias's apartment, and Mathias leaned in to kiss Pascal good-bye. It should have been a simple buss of lips to signify their parting, but Pascal couldn't stop at that. He needed more than that, and he needed it now. Fortunately Mathias didn't hesitate, throwing himself into the kiss with the same exuberance that had marked their day on the river, and Pascal felt himself going under again, giving in to the rise of passion between them. It would be so easy to push through the door, to follow Mathias into the shower, and make him late for work. Only the thought of what might ensue if that happened allowed him to pull back. He wouldn't be the cause of Mathias getting in trouble at work, not while he still needed the job at the bar to make ends meet.

"I'll see you on Tuesday."

"I'll talk to you tomorrow," Mathias countered. "I know you have to spend the day with your parents, but we can still talk before we go to work."

"I'll call you as soon as I get home," Pascal promised. "Be safe at the bar tonight."

"I always am," Mathias replied jauntily.

Pascal wasn't so sure about that given how they'd first met, but he kept those thoughts to himself. Mathias was an adult. He could make his own decisions.

CHAPTER 10

MATHIAS HAD been at Le Salon on Tuesday for two hours without a single customer in his section. That was bad enough. It would have been worse if anyone else were having better luck, but the bar was dead.

"Mathias," Adrien called.

Mathias headed toward the bar owner, hoping he hadn't done anything wrong without realizing it. He'd done his best to stay busy, but with so few customers, there hadn't been much to do.

"You don't have to stay," Adrien said. "You aren't earning tips because no one's here. Take the night off, catch up on your sleep. I know you're burning the candle at both ends."

Mathias thought about the lost income if he didn't get paid for the night, but honestly, most of his income came from tips, not from Adrien, so he wouldn't be losing much if he left, and tonight was Pascal's night off. Pascal hadn't come into the bar yet, but Mathias could head him off if he was planning on coming to Le Salon, and they could spend the night in.

In *him* if he had his way.

He all but ran back to the apartment building and took the steps two at a time all the way up to Pascal's door. He was a little out of breath by the time he got there, his heart pounding in his chest, but that was as much anticipation as exertion. He knocked on the door and waited, hoping Pascal was home. He hadn't mentioned meeting his friends for dinner when they'd texted earlier in the day, but that could have changed, and since Mathias was supposed to be working, Pascal wouldn't necessarily have let him know about the change in plans. He'd just have to hope for the best.

Pascal opened the door a minute later, and Mathias took a moment to just stare, his mouth watering as he raked his gaze over Pascal. Mathias had gotten used to seeing him in tailored slacks and a nice shirt, and Pascal had worn jeans and a sweatshirt when they went canoeing, but neither had prepared Mathias for the sheer wall of lust that slammed into him at the sight of Pascal in a pair of sleep pants and a threadbare T-shirt that had to be two sizes too small to hug his body that way. "Can I come in?"

Pascal took a step back, and Mathias took that as an invitation. He kicked the door closed as he passed and then pounced, kissing Pascal with all the fervor that had gone from a low-level awareness to a full-out burn in the span of ten seconds.

"I thought you were working tonight," Pascal gasped between kisses.

"I was," Mathias said. "The bar was dead. Adrien gave me the night off."

As far as Mathias was concerned, that was all they needed to say. He rubbed against Pascal, the friction on his erection driving him wild, and when he felt an answering hardness against his hip, he shifted so they pressed together. Pascal groaned and rutted back against him, giving Mathias all the encouragement he needed.

He worked his hands under the hem of Pascal's T-shirt. The soft cotton offered no real impediment to his touch, drifting upward as Mathias caressed the soft, hot skin of Pascal's back. He loved Pascal's body, all hard, lean muscle, not an ounce of fat anywhere, but broad-shouldered at the same time, the body of a man, not of a kid barely out of adolescence. One day Mathias would outgrow that stage.

Mathias stripped the T-shirt over Pascal's head and paused to look for a minute. He could all but see the doubt creeping through Pascal's mind at the momentary cessation, so he didn't stare as long as he might have at the crisp mat of silver and black hair covering Pascal's chest. He'd "look" with his fingers instead because he didn't want Pascal to have any doubt about how much Mathias wanted him.

With one hand, he pulled Pascal into a kiss, licking over Pascal's lips until they opened. As soon as they did, he delved inside, seeking Pascal's tongue with his own and enticing it to come out and play. As he'd hoped, Pascal quickly took control of the kiss, leaving Mathias free to enjoy and tantalize. He gave in eagerly when Pascal's tongue surged into his mouth in imitation of what Mathias fully intended Pascal to do with his cock before the night was over. He moaned encouragingly and ran his fingers through Pascal's short hair, ruffling it even if he didn't break the kiss to take in the surely delightful sight. He'd get a chance to look later, after they'd finished thoroughly mussing each other. Pascal bucked against him at the sound, so Mathias moaned again. When Pascal had the same reaction, Mathias filed that away for future reference. Pascal obviously appreciated Mathias's sounds of approval, which suited Mathias just fine. He'd never been good at staying quiet in bed. Wondering if he could seduce a few noises out of Pascal as well, he sucked on Pascal's tongue. He felt the answering groan all the way to his toes.

As much as Mathias loved kissing, it wouldn't be enough tonight. He was already too on edge to be satisfied with making out on the couch. He needed more than that, and he needed it now. Determined to speed things along, he ran his hands over the curve of Pascal's chest, appreciating the soft friction of hair over the hard bed of muscle.

Pascal arched into the touch with a soft gasp of his own. Mathias grinned into the kiss and repeated the caress. Almost immediately, Pascal pulled away, making Mathias wonder if he'd hit one of Pascal's sore spots, but Pascal simply grabbed the hem of the red T-shirt Mathias had worn to the bar that night and pulled it over his head.

Mathias lifted his arms to facilitate his disrobing. While he didn't want to stop touching Pascal, getting undressed was a necessary step if they were going to do more than kiss. The minute his hands were free of the cloth, Mathias grabbed Pascal's waist and pulled him close again, rubbing up against him. The rasp of chest hair against his sensitive nipples made him gasp. Pascal mimicked his stance and took control of their movements, dragging himself back and forth across Mathias's chest.

"Fuck," Mathias gasped.

"Isn't that why you came?" Pascal asked.

"I haven't come yet." Mathias thrust against Pascal's hip to emphasize his point, winning a groan from Pascal that he answered in kind. "You should do something about that."

Pascal ran his hand over the curve of Mathias's jeans-clad ass. "I would if I could get my hand inside these. They're so tight I wondered if they were painted on."

Mathias didn't hesitate, unbuttoning the waistband and shimmying the denim down over his hips. "Better?"

Pascal slid his hands inside Mathias's jeans and right past the waistband of his jockstrap to bare skin. Mathias didn't bother trying to stifle the noise that left his throat at that sensation. Pascal's hands were hot and hard, even as tentative as they were. Mathias didn't want tentative. He wanted Pascal to take charge, throw him onto the bed, and fuck him senseless. If that wasn't going to happen, though, he'd settle for pushing Pascal onto the bed and riding him until they were both senseless.

With that goal in mind, he shimmied again until his jeans were around his knees. He toed off his shoes and stepped clear of his pants. Then he grabbed Pascal's sleep pants and pushed those down as well. "Bed?" he suggested.

Pascal seemed startled by the question, but Mathias grabbed his hand and pulled him deeper into the apartment toward the open door to Pascal's bedroom. Pascal followed willingly enough. When Mathias glanced over his shoulder, Pascal had his gaze fixed on Mathias's bare ass framed by the black straps of his jock. Mathias wasn't above swishing his hips a bit as he walked to keep Pascal's focus where he wanted it.

He could see the need in Pascal's eyes when they reached the bedroom and he turned to face his soon-to-be lover, but Pascal still didn't make a move. Deciding he'd had enough, Mathias pushed Pascal backward onto the bed and straddled his hips. "What's a boy got to do to get a little attention around here?" he teased as he rocked his ass against Pascal's groin. "Beg?"

Pascal bucked up beneath him, his cock slotting enticingly into Mathias's crease. He reached out and snapped the waistband of the jock. "Get rid of this, and we'll talk about it."

Mathias lifted up enough to strip the last of his clothes away, leaving them both completely bare, and then settled back across Pascal's body. "Mmmm… perfect."

He ran his hands over Pascal's chest again, taking the time to look as well as touch now that he had Pascal naked and pinned beneath him. Pascal didn't have any interest in getting away, if the way he stroked Mathias's skin in return was any indication.

Before long, looking and touching weren't enough. Mathias slid down enough that he could lower his head to Pascal's chest and lick over the nub of flesh peeking out from his chest hair. Pascal undulated beneath him, encouraging Mathias to continue. He angled his hips enough to get a hand between their bodies as well so he could stroke Pascal's cock. The whiff of musk that reached his nose made his mouth water, so he abandoned one treat for another. Pascal bucked up into his mouth when he closed his lips around the tip of his erection, but Mathias had expected the motion and moved with it so Pascal didn't choke him. Pascal tasted salty and a little bitter, but not enough to stop Mathias from what he was doing, not when Pascal was gasping and moaning, his hands scrabbling for purchase in the sheets.

Mathias took his time, lingering over the head and working the foreskin with his tongue. Pascal bucked up again, and this time, Mathias let him press deeper, relishing the feel of the thick shaft against his tongue and the way the head nudged the back of his throat. He pulled back a bit, took a deep breath, and plunged his head down, taking Pascal all the way in.

Pascal moaned and jerked into Mathias's mouth, fucking deeper. Mathias followed the movement and swallowed as the head of Pascal's cock pushed into his throat. Pascal bellowed out his pleasure. Mathias would have smiled if his mouth hadn't been full. As it was, he cupped Pascal's balls and rolled them against his palm as he bobbed his head in counterpoint to Pascal's thrusts. With his other hand, he squeezed the base of his own erection to keep himself under control. He didn't want to come like a kid with his first crush. He wanted Pascal to see him as an adult, an equal, age difference aside.

He worked Pascal hard until he could feel Pascal's thighs start to tremble on either side of his head. Only then did he pull off and crawl up over Pascal's body. "Do you have supplies?"

"Now's a fine time to ask," Pascal said shakily. Mathias nuzzled into the curve of his shoulder. He had a condom in his wallet, but it had been too long since he'd last bottomed to take Pascal with nothing but spit as lube. Hopefully Pascal would have something. Even if he didn't do casual sex, he might have some for self-pleasure. And if not, Mathias could go back to what he'd been doing. It wouldn't be the same as having Pascal inside him, but it would do for tonight.

"I wasn't exactly planning this when I got dressed for work tonight," he replied. "I can get dressed and—"

"There's lube in the drawer, and I think I still have a box of condoms in the bathroom. I don't know how old they are, but not more than a couple of years."

The one in Mathias's wallet was newer than that. "Find the lube. I'll get a condom."

He walked back into the living room to get his wallet out of his jeans. He could feel Pascal's eyes on him as he went, sending a rush of power through him. This a-fucking-mazing man couldn't take his eyes off him. He rifled through his wallet and found the foil-wrapped packet. He checked quickly that it hadn't torn or punctured, but it appeared intact, so he carried it back to the bedroom.

Pascal had moved while Mathias was out of the room. He lazed against the headboard, his eyes dark with lust as he watched Mathias come back toward the bed. Mathias started to crawl back over Pascal to his earlier spot, but Pascal caught his arm and rolled him onto his back. "My turn," he murmured.

Mathias lay back and grinned at him. "My pleasure."

"It will be."

Mathias bit back a moan at the thrill that shot through him from the promise in Pascal's voice. He'd pushed Pascal into taking control. Now he'd reap the benefits of having an older, experienced lover. Pascal pinned him in place with a kiss, deep and hungry and claiming, until Mathias whimpered a little from the sheer desperation for more. His chest ached with need and his legs twitched restlessly, trying to find purchase on the bed, but Pascal stilled them with his own leg across Mathias's knees. Passion churned in his gut and clawed at his throat until he wanted to scream with it, and all Pascal had done was kiss him. He'd never survive the rest.

"Relax," Pascal whispered against his ear.

How the hell was he supposed to do that? He was strung tight as the bowstring on his dad's hunting bow, the one Mathias had never managed to pull all the way. Mathias cried out when Pascal brushed his fingers over the tip of his erection.

"I'll come," Mathias gasped. "Just… just get me… ready."

Pascal shook his head and took Mathias's mouth in another deep, devouring kiss as he found the spot on the underside of Mathias's cock that robbed him of all control. He came with a shout that was lost in the depths of Pascal's mouth, his cock spurting all over his belly. His cheeks burned with embarrassment coupled with his continuing need. He'd wanted to stay in control, but all it had taken was the touch of Pascal's hand.

"I'm sorry," he said when Pascal broke the kiss.

"I'm not," Pascal drawled. "You're young. You've got another one in you. And this way, I can take my time and play."

Mathias swallowed hard at the thought. "What did you have in mind?"

Pascal's wicked grin sent renewed need curing through Mathias's stomach. He slicked his fingers and nudged Mathias's hip. "Roll over. I've been dreaming about your ass."

Mathias whimpered a little at the thought as he rolled onto his stomach. The sheets were cool against his flushed skin. He pushed up on one elbow so he could watch Pascal's face. Pascal's gaze was fixed on the curve of his ass. As far as Mathias was concerned, it was his best feature. His upper body was still skinny, more boy than man, but he'd been groped enough at the bar to know his butt caught men's eyes. Pascal bent and nuzzled the curve of one cheek before biting sharply at the sensitive skin where his thigh met his ass. Mathias cried out in surprise, but when Pascal looked up at him questioningly, Mathias smiled. It had caught him off guard, but the sting was fading, leaving a tingly pleasure in its place. Pascal grinned back at him for a moment before returning his attention to the tender patch of skin. Mathias braced himself for another bite, but Pascal kept his teeth behind his lips, mouthing at the smooth surface instead. He had finally started to relax into the sensation when Pascal slipped a finger between his cheeks and pressed against his hole. Mathias reared up off the bed with a sharp gasp.

"Relax," Pascal urged.

Relax, my foot, Mathias thought. He'd never manage to relax with Pascal's mouth on him and his finger inside him. Not happening.

Pascal left his finger where it was, resting inside Mathias until he settled onto the bed again. Even then he left it barely inside Mathias's passage, one knuckle deep, just enough for Mathias to feel him without doing anything to him. Mathias squirmed, trying to get some friction on his cock or Pascal's finger deeper inside against his prostate or something.

Pascal shifted onto his knees so he could have one hand free and started kneading Mathias's ass soothingly. That wasn't any better as far as Mathias was concerned. He wanted Pascal to move, to stretch him open with his fingers so he could pound into him with his cock. He angled his head so he could see Pascal. Had Pascal lost interest in him now that he wasn't touching him? But no, Pascal's cock was still hard against his body. Whatever the delay was, it wasn't lack of interest.

"What are you waiting for?" Mathias whined.

"For you to relax," Pascal said. "We aren't in a hurry."

Mathias was tempted to argue that point, but he wanted Pascal to fuck him, not pull away to talk, so he subsided onto the bed, doing his best to relax despite the need riding him. If they were just starting out, maybe he'd appreciate the gesture. Or if he'd come down from his first orgasm before Pascal starting working on the second. But he hadn't. He was just as wound up, just as interested in what came next as he'd been when he walked in the door. It hadn't even taken the edge off. It just made him desperate for more.

He didn't know what sign Pascal was waiting for, but Mathias must have given it because finally he moved his finger, the slightest of rocking motions, barely enough to feel with the lube easing the way. Mathias spread his legs wider to give Pascal better access, and when that didn't encourage him to move faster, he reached back with one hand and spread his cheeks so Pascal could see as well as feel what he was doing.

"Stop tempting me," Pascal said with a light swat to Mathias's ass.

"Why?" Mathias asked. "You want it. I want it. Why should I pretend otherwise?"

Pascal didn't answer, but he did push his finger deeper into Mathias's passage, although not quite deep enough to find his prostate. Mathias squirmed on the bed, wishing he could get to his knees so he could rock back against Pascal's hand. He hissed at the shock of cold lube as Pascal added a second finger alongside the first, the chill another layer of sensation on top of the stretch he relished for what it promised. Pascal wouldn't take this much care prepping him if he didn't intend to give Mathias what he wanted before the night was over.

Pascal twisted his fingers inside Mathias's body, deepening the stretch on his guardian muscle. Mathias humped the mattress and pushed back onto Pascal's fingers. Pascal moved with him, keeping his fingers from penetrating any deeper.

"Tease!" Mathias said, his voice breaking on a sob.

Immediately Pascal drove his fingers as deep as they would go and pressed them unerringly against Mathias's prostate. Mathias keened with the explosion of need along his nerves. He'd had lovers play with his ass before. He wasn't a virgin by any stretch of the imagination, but he'd never felt anything so intense. How the hell did Pascal make everything more powerful? He'd have to wait to get an answer because Pascal played mercilessly over his sweet spot, ratcheting up his need until he was gasping for breath, unable to more than whimper with each pass over his gland.

Mathias rocked back against Pascal's hand, begging silently for more. Instead, the touch disappeared. Mathias whined a protest, but Pascal rubbed his back soothingly. "We're not done," he said, and his voice sounded nearly as desperate as Mathias felt. It was little consolation as Mathias lay there panting, wondering what came next. Pascal scissored his fingers, stretching Mathias's hole almost to the point of pain, but just as Mathias opened his mouth to protest, Pascal released the pressure and returned to fucking Mathias with his fingers. When he relaxed beneath the curling pleasure, Pascal did it again. Mathias hissed in protest as soon as it started this time. Pascal eased off almost immediately and pressed back in with three fingers to tantalize Mathias's prostate again. Mathias let out a shout, amazed to feel a second climax building at the base of his spine.

"Now," he begged. "I won't make it a third round."

Pascal pulled his fingers free. The moment he did, Mathias started to roll to his back again. Pascal stopped him with one firm hand. "Don't move."

Mathis frowned. He wanted to see Pascal's face, but he'd recognized the command in Pascal's implacable tone. If he pushed back, he might not get what he wanted, and he was too desperate now to take that risk. They'd have other nights. He'd see Pascal's face then. He pulled his knees up beneath him and arched his back. If Pascal wanted to look at his ass while they fucked, he'd put on the most enticing display possible.

To his relief, Pascal fell on him like a starving man and thrust home in one strong push. Mathias cried out in delight as he was filled with Pascal's long, hard shaft. He didn't know if he could have lasted through another bout of Pascal's drawn-out teasing. It had been all he could do not to come from Pascal's fingers inside him. Now that it was Pascal's cock stretching him open, he wouldn't last long.

Pascal pegged his prostate with every pass, driving the breath from Mathias's lungs and every coherent thought from his head. He hung there, head down, breath sawing in and out as Pascal commandeered his body completely. He whined, deep in his throat, but he couldn't put words to his protest. He needed to come. He needed to breathe. He needed....

His orgasm blindsided him, his vision whiting out as all strength deserted him. His elbows gave out, and he hit the bed face-first, only his hips, caught between Pascal's hands, still raised off the bed. He gasped again as Pascal kept pistoning into him until he thought he'd go mad from the mixture of pleasure from his prostate and pain from the constriction of his muscles. When he thought he couldn't take it a second longer, Pascal thrust one last time and then stilled. He released his grip on Mathias's hips and let him sink fully onto the bed. Mathias had the stray thought that he shouldn't fall asleep, but he was too sated to move. He'd get up in a while and go back to his apartment.

CHAPTER 11

THE SOUND of his phone alarm going off roused Mathias from a deep sleep and the most pleasant dream. He'd gone to Pascal's apartment, and Pascal had taken him to bed and….

He rolled to find his phone, only to encounter a hard body in bed with him. Oh God, it hadn't been a dream. The ache in his ass was all the proof he needed of that, even without opening his eyes to see Pascal lying next to him. He scrambled out of the bed, trying to find his phone before the alarm woke Pascal too, but he couldn't remember where he'd left it in the rush to bed the night before. The sound drew him back into the living room. He finally silenced the alarm with a groan. Bad enough he'd come by unexpectedly last night and jumped Pascal—Pascal hadn't complained about that—now he'd fallen asleep in Pascal's bed and woken him up early with his alarm. What an auspicious start.

He'd get his things and go. Pascal could fall back asleep, hopefully, and they could talk tonight when he got off work, or this weekend if they couldn't find time to talk before then. It didn't have to be a disaster. Pascal could have roused him last night and sent him home if he'd really wanted Mathias to leave.

His jockstrap was in the bedroom. He could leave it, but that would be both rude and uncomfortable. In a loose pair of jeans, maybe it would be okay, but not in his bar jeans. He'd never get the zipper over his dick without scraping it raw. He'd be walking funny enough at work today without adding that to the mix. There was nothing for it. He'd have to go get it.

He took a deep breath and walked back into the bedroom. With luck, Pascal had already fallen back asleep. He tiptoed toward the bed. He'd tossed his jockstrap from there, not that he knew where it had landed, but he had to start somewhere. He'd gotten four steps into the room when Pascal flipped on the bedside lamp.

Mathias flinched at the sudden light. "Sorry. I didn't mean to fall asleep last night and wake you up this morning. I just need to get my jockstrap, and I'll be out of your way."

Pascal nodded, obviously not awake, but didn't say anything. He followed Mathias with his eyes as he searched for his jockstrap, but Mathias couldn't decipher his expression. As good as last night had felt, he wondered now if it had been a mistake. Pascal wasn't yelling at him to hurry up, but neither was he smiling or doing anything to make the very awkward situation more comfortable.

Mathias found his jockstrap finally in the far corner of the room, half-hidden beneath the chest of drawers. How had it ended up there? It didn't matter. He'd found it. He could get dressed and get to work.

"I have to go. I'll be late to work if I don't hurry. I'll call you later?" He had to salvage something out of this.

"I have to open tonight. I'll already be at the restaurant when you get off work."

"I could call you during my lunch break," Mathias offered.

"If you want to."

The knots in Mathias's stomach tightened at the indifference in Pascal's voice. Had he done something wrong last night? Had he been that bad a lay? Or had he finally given Pascal what he really wanted and Pascal was done with him?

He didn't have time to deal with this right now. He was already running late—normally he'd be done with his shower by now. He wanted to kiss Pascal good-bye at least, but the closed expression on his face made that less tempting than usual. Giving up, he went into the living room, pulled his clothes on, and left. He made sure the door shut behind him, but Pascal would have to lock it from the inside if he wanted it locked.

Mathias hurried downstairs to his apartment and into the shower. He could skip breakfast and grab coffee from the break room at the bank. That would save him a few minutes. Even so, he'd have to hope he was lucky with the trains.

The hot water stung as it ran down his back, but he needed it to wake up since he didn't have time to make coffee. His backside ached, a reminder of everything Pascal had done the night before. If they hadn't parted so awkwardly this morning, he'd relish the reminder of how they'd spent the night. It had been everything Mathias dreamed. Pascal was as masterful a lover as Mathias had known he would be, and every touch had been perfect.

So what the hell had gone wrong?

He didn't have time to think about this now. He needed to get out of the shower, get dressed, and get to work, because it would just be the icing on an already shitty cake if he was late. He finished in the shower and got out the door as fast as he could.

His luck held—his bad luck, that is—and he just missed the train that would have gotten him to work on time. He shifted restlessly from one foot to another as he waited for the next one. His mind raced despite his best effort not to think about Pascal and everything that had happened the night before and that morning. If the morning had gone differently, he wouldn't mind the memories of the night. It was the damn awkwardness and Pascal's odd silence that tainted the otherwise good feelings.

The next train finally came, but moving toward work did nothing to help Mathias's mindset. He hoped he could get his act together at work because he wouldn't do anyone any good if he stayed this distracted all day. He just didn't understand. The sex had been stellar. Pascal had wrung two orgasms out of him like it was child's play. Mathias couldn't remember the last time he'd had sex that good.

He'd maybe been a little selfish, falling asleep the way he did, but Pascal hadn't kicked him out, either, and he'd stayed awake long enough to deal with the condom, so he could have woken Mathias up.

Had he been too selfish in not doing more to return the pleasure Pascal lavished on him? He'd tried at first, until Pascal had rolled him onto his stomach and taken control. He hadn't given Mathias time to breathe after that. Should he have tried harder? He could have, but Pascal had stopped him the one time he'd tried. Not that he'd minded, really. He would've like to see Pascal's face when he ca—

Oh shit. Had Pascal come? He'd stopped, but Mathias had just assumed. He wouldn't have stopped otherwise, would he? Except that Mathias had hardly given him much choice, coming to his apartment and jumping him the minute the door opened, even knowing Pascal wasn't ready for them to have sex. He hadn't said no. He'd responded to Mathias's overtures, but that wasn't the same thing, not when he'd made it clear he didn't want to rush.

Oh God, what had he done?

He stumbled out of the train and up the stairs toward work, only peripherally aware of his surroundings. No one stopped him as he made his way to his desk, but that counted as the only blessing of the morning.

"WHAT'S UP with you today?" Louis asked when he cornered Mathias at lunch. Mathias had managed to avoid talking with him all morning, using calls and meetings as an excuse to postpone the inevitable. His boss hadn't seen him come in late that morning, but Louis had, and he'd want an explanation for that, if nothing else.

Mathias shrugged. "It hasn't been a very good day."

That was the understatement of the year, but he wasn't ready to say more than that. If he had a better idea of what had been going on in Pascal's head that morning, he might have felt differently. Louis had been a good friend and sounding board in more than just work, but he couldn't very well explain a situation he didn't understand himself.

"You've been busy, but it didn't look like things you couldn't handle," Louis said.

"It's not work," Mathias replied. "Other than running late this morning."

Louis frowned. "About that… if working at the bar is going to make you late, you need to seriously consider where your priorities lie. I know all your reasons for it, and I know it's only temporary, but you don't want to endanger the job that will make it temporary because of it."

"I wasn't at the bar last night," Mathias said. "Or rather, Adrien sent me home early because it was dead."

"Then what's the problem?" Louis asked. "You're usually wide-awake and full of energy if you've had a night off."

This was the problem with a mentor who paid so much attention. He couldn't hide behind lingering tiredness because Louis would see right through that lie. "I slept fine." He'd slept better than he could remember sleeping since he moved to Montréal. Between the sex and the exhaustion, he'd passed out and not moved until his alarm went off. Pascal's bed was comfortable, and Pascal's presence had been soothing last night. This morning on the other hand…. "It was the morning that wasn't fine."

"I can't help you if you don't talk to me," Louis said.

"I'm not sure you could help me regardless," Mathias said. "It doesn't have anything to do with work, either job."

"Did you and Pascal have a fight?" Louis pressed.

Mathias sighed. So much for not talking to Louis about it. "I don't know. Last night was his night off, so when Adrien let me leave early, I went to see him. One thing led to another, and, well…." He trailed off, not sure how to explain everything that had happened and all his fears about how Pascal might have viewed it. "Let's just say I didn't go home last night."

Louis grinned and waggled his eyebrows at Mathias. "That sounds promising. Did you oversleep?"

"No, my alarm went off, but it was awkward. Really awkward. He didn't ask me to stay. I sort of passed out in his bed. Hell, I don't even know if he actually wanted me there in the first place. It seemed so easy as I was walking there last night. And this morning nothing seemed easy. And there wasn't time to talk, or I'd have been even later than I already was."

"You can talk to him tonight," Louis said. "I'm sure it's nothing."

Mathias summoned a smile to acknowledge Louis's comment and left it at that. It wasn't nothing, but he couldn't explain all of that to Louis. "I told him I'd call him on my lunch break. I should go do that before I'm out of time."

"Oh, of course," Louis said.

Mathias escaped the break room and went outside. He didn't want anyone to overhear the upcoming conversation, but better a random stranger than one of his colleagues. The sun shone brightly overhead, in stark contrast to his mood, but at least it kept the temperature high enough that he didn't need a coat over his suit jacket.

"Hello?"

"I wasn't sure you'd answer," Mathias blurted out when Pascal answered the phone.

"I'm not that petty," Pascal replied.

The answer hardly reassured Mathias, but as long as they were talking, he'd hold on to hope.

"I'm sorry about this morning," Mathias said. "I should have gone back to my apartment last night so I wouldn't wake you up."

"I could have woken you last night," Pascal replied. "No harm done."

Mathias might have believed that if Pascal's voice hadn't sounded so stilted. "I know you'll be at work already when I get home, but what time do you get off tonight? I'd like to see you."

"Too late for you," Pascal replied. "You have to be at the bank early. You should go to sleep as soon as you finish at Le Salon. I'll see you Saturday like we planned."

Mathias was glad Pascal hadn't canceled their date for Saturday, but that was only mildly reassuring in the face of all his doubts. He couldn't have that conversation with Pascal over the phone. He needed to see Pascal's face.

"Yes, I'll see you then," Mathias replied. "But I'll try to call or text before then too."

"If your schedule permits," Pascal said, and the words that had always seemed so considerate of his crazy life suddenly felt like a dismissal. He wanted to rant and rave, but it wouldn't do any good when he couldn't see Pascal's expression. Maybe it was still the same consideration, or maybe it was a dismissal. Yesterday he would have said it was consideration, but that was before Mathias forgot all consideration of Pascal's wishes and barged into his apartment, unexpected and uninvited. He still hoped he wasn't unwelcome, but now he wasn't even sure about that.

Chapter 12

PASCAL STARED down at the phone in his hand as if he could find the answers to all the questions in the universe hidden in its depths, but the screen stayed resolutely black after the call with Mathias. The incredibly awkward, stilted call with Mathias to go along with the incredibly awkward, stilted morning-after. He should have put a stop to it the minute Mathias knocked on his door last night. He should have insisted Mathias go home and get a good night's sleep in his own bed instead of giving in to the temptation Mathias represented. But it had felt so good to be wanted that way—too good, but that was a problem of an entirely different nature. Mathias was this bright, shining young thing with enough passion to burn them both to cinders, and Pascal had gone down without a fight. That might not have been a problem if he'd had an exit strategy, but then Mathias had fallen asleep, so clearly exhausted that Pascal couldn't make himself wake him. He shouldn't have let it go so far. He should have stopped after the hand job, let Mathias return the favor, and called it a night.

He'd broken every tenet he'd set up for their relationship, and he'd done it at the slightest hint of provocation. Yes, Mathias had looked good enough to eat in his tight T-shirt and tighter jeans, but Pascal had been resisting that kind of temptation ever since he and Robert decided to make a real go of it. He shouldn't have cracked so easily. It was too much, too soon. He'd thought Mathias understood that. Maybe not agreed with him, but accepted it. Apparently he'd been wrong, and his own willpower had evaporated at the sight of Mathias's sweet ass framed by the jockstrap. He was only human, and some temptations were too much to resist.

He closed his eyes and reveled in the memory of Mathias's hands and mouth on him, the way Mathias had taken him in and urged him on. He had gotten used to thinking of himself as too old to start over—the silver at his temples was more than mirrored by the silver on his chest—but Mathias hadn't looked at him like he was old. Mathias had reached for him like a starving man at a banquet, and Pascal had given and given and given. What else could he do when he was as starved as Mathias had been?

That didn't make it a good idea. None of it had been a good idea. All the way back to letting Mathias convince him to try a different drink, it had been one bad idea after another. He could be excused that weakness. Mathias had been relentless in his pursuit, when he wasn't being adorably awkward in his youth, and Pascal could admit to feeling flattered by the attention. What man wouldn't be flattered to be the object of affection of a much younger man who could have anyone he wanted? Mathias deserved so much more than Pascal could offer, though. He wasn't young and smooth and full of life. He was middle-aged—approaching old if René was to be believed—and battered and frozen inside.

The only thing they had in common besides their address was working as waiters, and even that barely counted when he thought of the differences in where they worked and why, and of where Mathias was really going in his life. He'd known what would happen if they had sex. He knew himself well enough to know that casual wasn't really an option between them when Mathias burned so brightly with everything Pascal no longer had. He'd delayed it, hoping things would reach the inevitable point of petering out before they ended up in bed together. He could handle a few kisses, even making out on the couch, but he had never been a love 'em and leave 'em kind of guy, not even when he was Mathias's age. Sure, he'd played around a little, fumbling experiments in darkened corners of bars and bathhouses, but his insistence on actually caring about his bed partners before he slept with them had probably saved his life, unlike so many of his friends who had died of AIDS. He could count on one hand the men he'd had full-on sex with, and that included Mathias.

The sudden buzzing of his phone startled him. For a minute, he hoped—feared—it was Mathias calling him back to demand an explanation or to rail at him for being an idiot, but then the name popped up, and he cursed under his breath. He was supposed to meet René and Benjamin at noon. It was twelve thirty, and he was still at his apartment.

He could make his excuses and bow out, but they'd want to know why. Of course if he had to have it out with them, doing it as his apartment would be better than doing it out in public.

Not going to make it today. Sorry, he texted back.

His phone buzzed again moments later. *No excuses. You come to us or we come to you.*

He cursed again, louder this time. He wasn't up for this today. *Fine. Come here when you're done with lunch.*

That would give him time to shower so he didn't smell like sex when they walked in. Then again, as well as they knew him, they'd probably take one look at him and know what he and Mathias had done.

He was so screwed.

He had managed to shower and get dressed by the time he heard a knock on his door. He opened it to let René and Benjamin inside, ignoring their questioning looks.

"We brought you lunch," René said. "We figured you hadn't eaten and would want something before you went into work tonight."

"Thanks." Pascal took the carryout bag and set it on the table, but he made no move to open it. He wasn't hungry.

"What's going on?" Benjamin asked when Pascal didn't say anything else.

Pascal shrugged.

"You didn't have a date with Mathias, so you haven't had a fight unless it was over the phone," René said. "Is your mother doing worse?"

"Not that I've heard. It was Sylvie's turn to visit them last weekend, but she would've told me if things had deteriorated."

"You've been so happy recently," Benjamin said. "You were finally getting out from under the shadow of grief, and now you're all weighted down again. Whatever it is, you can tell us. We can't help if we don't know what's going on."

"I slept with Mathias," he blurted out.

Both his friends' eyebrows jumped nearly to their hairlines. Pascal might have laughed at their comical expressions if he weren't so miserable.

"Was the sex that bad?" René joked. Benjamin elbowed him, making Pascal snort.

"It wasn't bad. It just wasn't a good idea."

"I've seen your boyfriend," René insisted. "There's no way sex with him could be a bad idea unless he's a bad lover."

He hadn't been a bad lover. He'd been everything Pascal could have hoped for in a lover—eager, passionate, giving but just as willing to take. The image of Mathias's flustered face after he came the first time was etched into Pascal's mind, and the way he'd rolled to his stomach, giving Pascal unrestricted access to play was enough to have him hardening again from memory alone. None of that made it less of a bad idea.

"He's not the problem. I am," Pascal said.

"How do you figure that?" Benjamin asked seriously, elbowing René again when he started to say something.

"I don't even know where to start."

René opened his mouth again but shut it at Benjamin's sharp look.

Pascal ran a hand over his short hair, trying to put into words all the doubts assailing him. "Right now, he's twenty-four and I'm forty-eight. It's an age gap, but I'm still young enough to keep up with him. What happens in a few years when he's still young and suddenly he's saddled with this old man?"

"Harrison Ford is twenty-five years older than you are. I wouldn't kick him out of bed," René said. Benjamin glared at him. "Just throwing that out there."

"Not helping," Benjamin said. "Have you asked him about the age difference?"

"Not in so many words, although he's said more than once that he likes older men," Pascal admitted, although the comparison reassured him somewhat, because René was certainly right. "He's so damn young. Sometimes I feel ancient just looking at him."

"Turn it around," Benjamin said. "He'll keep you young."

Pascal chuckled. He certainly hadn't felt his age when he'd been balls-deep in Mathias the night before. He couldn't remember the last time he'd felt that good. Then they'd fallen asleep, and this morning had happened. He couldn't remember the last time he'd felt that bad. "Or drive me into an early grave."

"But what a way to go!"

Pascal snorted. He could certainly think of worse ways to go than from trying to keep up with a lover half his age, but that assumed Mathias would want to stay with him that long. He had so much going for him. He didn't need Pascal tying him down.

"I know we met him at Le Salon, but he's so much more than just a waiter," Pascal said. "I look at him and see this bright kid with an amazing future. He's going somewhere. Maybe it won't be where he thinks he's going right now, but no way he's going to be satisfied with waiting tables all his life. And when he's middle or upper management at a big bank or other firm, he's not going to want to be with me."

"What's wrong with you?" René demanded loyally. "You help run that restaurant. You're middle management at least."

"Thanks, but no one else will see it that way," Pascal said with a sad smile. "Even Robert didn't see it that way half the time, and he helped me get the job in the first place."

"Has Mathias said anything to make you think he feels that way?" Benjamin asked.

Pascal tried to remember a specific instance, but he couldn't put his finger on anything. "No."

"Then don't put words in his mouth."

"Put something else there instead," René suggested.

Pascal flushed with the memory of Mathias closing his lips around his cock. God, he was pathetic. He was too old to be popping a boner at every sexual innuendo out of Rene's mouth.

"I think he's already done that," Benjamin observed mildly. "That hasn't stopped him from sitting here fretting."

"You make me sound like a teenage girl," Pascal grumbled.

"If the shoe fits…."

"I haven't told him about Robert."

Benjamin sighed. "You're forty-eight. He can't possibly imagine you haven't had relationships before him. Are you obsessing over his past lovers? Because that was no virgin ass you tapped last night."

"How would you know?" Pascal retorted automatically. Mathias hadn't been a virgin. He'd been too sure of himself for that, not that it was any of Benjamin's business.

"You don't live on rue Sainte-Catherine and work in a gay bar at his age if you aren't comfortable with who you are, and you don't get comfortable with who you are without experimenting," Benjamin said with a shrug. "You didn't answer my question."

"No, he's with me now, not them. That's all I care about," Pascal said.

"Then why do you think hearing about Robert will matter to him?" Benjamin asked.

"Maybe it won't, but I have to tell him," Pascal insisted. "He has to understand what he's getting into."

"Oh, for Christ's sake, you make it sound like you have some communicable disease because Robert died of cancer," René snapped. "And don't give me that look. He was my friend too, and I miss him terribly. Not the way you do, but I do miss him. But you've mourned long enough. You've got this really cute, apparently quite smart and interesting man interested in you, and I'll be damned if I sit here and watch you screw it up because you've got some bug up your ass."

"And how are you going to stop me from doing that?" Pascal asked, smiling for what felt like the first time since Mathias's alarm woke them up that morning.

"No idea, but I'll come up with something," René muttered.

It wouldn't be that easy, no matter what René thought. He needed to talk to Mathias, a real conversation, not the stilted nonsense of that morning or their lunch-break phone call. His stomach curled with dread at the thought. He didn't honestly see how anything good could come of it, of them. They were too different, but he owed it to Mathias to resolve it in person rather than just let it slide away into nothing.

"I know that look," Benjamin said before Pascal's thoughts could spiral downward again. "You've already written him off in your head. You're so convinced this can't work that you aren't even willing to fight for it. I thought better of you."

The disappointment in Benjamin's voice stung. "What else can I do? None of this is stuff I can change."

"None of it needs to change," Benjamin said. "What needs to change is your attitude about it. The age difference is real. You're not going to get younger. He's not going to suddenly be older. That's fact. What isn't fact is whether the age difference is a problem. He's going into banking. You help manage a four-star restaurant in the business district. That's fact. That doesn't mean he's ashamed of you or that you're going to somehow hold him back. You were in a long-term, serious relationship that only ended when Robert died. That's fact. Nothing about that keeps you from loving again. Nor is it a reason for someone else not to love you. If anything, it's a point in your favor that you still care so deeply for him."

It sounded so simple when Benjamin said it, but Pascal knew better than to think the reality would be anything close to easy.

"What do you have to lose?" Benjamin asked more gently.

Everything, he wanted to say, but that was too pat an answer because he hadn't known Mathias long enough for him to be that deeply woven into the fabric of Pascal's life. Mathias's interest, however fleeting it might end up being, was undeniably real. He'd jumped Pascal last night, not the other way around. He'd clearly wanted to be exactly where they ended up. He'd come twice, so his enjoyment wasn't in question. The problem lay in letting himself become more invested than he already was in a relationship that had no guarantee of lasting. He'd already had his heart shattered once when Robert died. Even if Mathias wanted the pieced-together shards that were left for the moment, when he moved on, it would destroy what little peace Pascal had been able to salvage.

"I know that look," René groused. "You're brooding again. Stop it."

"I see too many ways for everything to go wrong and not enough ways for it to work out," Pascal admitted.

"I've never known a relationship to start any other way," Benjamin said. "Nobody said it would be easy, and maybe it won't work out, but what if it does? What if instead of coming home to an empty apartment every night, you got to come home to Mathias? What if instead of living vicariously through your romance novels—yes, we know about your secret stash—you actually had a romance of your own to enjoy? Just think about it, okay? And talk to Mathias about it. Maybe you're right and you can't work out all the hurdles, but maybe I'm right and you can be happy again."

"We had a date planned for Saturday."

"Good. Call him right now and tell him it's still on," Benjamin said.

"He's at work. I can't call now."

"Then text him," René said. "You're not an idiot, despite the way you're acting. Because you're right about one thing: he *is* young, which means he's going to blow this even more out of proportion than you have, and if he thinks you don't want him anymore, he's going to work himself up so much that Saturday will be a fiasco."

Pascal wasn't sure what he could say that would help.

"Tell him you're looking forward to seeing him. Make a suggestion about what you can do on the date. Something that isn't the conversation you need to have."

"We'd been talking about biking up to Mont Royal," Pascal said.

"Good. Tell him that."

Pascal picked up his phone and stared at the screen for a moment before pulling up the last text from Mathias. He took a deep breath and sent a new note: *Want to go biking this weekend? The leaves should be starting to turn.*

They could talk when they got back, if Mathias accepted his suggestion.

"Happy now?" Pascal asked Benjamin.

"As happy as I'm likely to be until you get this worked out," Benjamin said. "Now, don't work it up into an insurmountable obstacle in your head between now and then. Don't doom yourself to failure over nothing."

It wouldn't be nothing, but Benjamin wouldn't be swayed, and Pascal was tired of talking about it. "I'll do my best."

MATHIAS GLANCED down when his phone buzzed. He wasn't really supposed to send or read personal texts during work hours, but he couldn't stop himself from reaching for the phone. Pascal's name flashed at him, so he opened the message app and read the note. It wasn't long or romantic or even anything new, not really. They'd already agreed to keep the date they had planned on Saturday, but it felt momentous nonetheless. Pascal still wanted to make plans with him, not just tell him to get the hell out, and that settled Mathias enough that he could smile and type out a response.

Biking sounds great if the weather stays good.

He tucked his phone back in his jacket pocket and went back to the e-mail he'd been writing, a smile on his face.

CHAPTER 13

PASCAL CAME out of the kitchen on Thursday night with an order for an early table and checked automatically to see if he had any new customers. They didn't have a lot of reservations, either because of the storms that had blustered through town off and on all day or because it was Thursday, but they usually got decent referral traffic from the surrounding hotels on nights like this. The free shuttle was a big draw when the weather was bad. To his surprise, Martine, Hélène, Camille, and Nicole had come in while he was in the kitchen. He delivered the meal in his hand with his best professional smile in place, then turned toward his ladies, his smile morphing into a smirk.

Hélène looked up as he started across the room and met his smirk with one of her own. She was wearing red lipstick tonight, a change from her usual muted palette. He wondered what had inspired the change. He'd have to be sure to compliment her on it, regardless of the reason, because the bright color complemented her black hair perfectly.

"How's our favorite waiter?" she asked when Pascal moved within earshot.

His smile slipped despite his efforts to keep it in place. He didn't even bother hoping they wouldn't notice.

Camille pushed out the extra chair at the table. "Want to sit down and tell us about it?"

"I shouldn't," Pascal said. "I have other tables besides yours tonight. I didn't see your names on the reservations."

"We didn't make a reservation," Martine said. "We had reservations for next week, but an event came up at the last minute, and I wouldn't have been able to make it, so we took the chance on coming in tonight. And you don't have to sit down now, but you do have to tell us about it. We can't help if we don't know what's wrong."

He doubted they could help even if he told them every last detail, but that wouldn't deter them. "I don't even know where to start."

"With why you aren't still over the moon in love with your boy like you were the last time we were here," Nicole said, "but you can think about it while you bring us a round of cosmos. You've been so happy lately. We hate seeing you sad now."

That brought a real smile to his face, even as he reeled from the rest of her statement, because he couldn't hear them talk about how much they cared and not smile. They had been with him through so much. "Four cosmos coming up. Think about appetizers and dinner while I'm getting those."

He placed their order at the bar and retreated to the restroom for a moment. Anywhere else and someone might come up to him with a question. Normally he relished his role as head waiter and the chance it gave him to mentor the younger waiters, but he needed to breathe—and think—without interruption long enough to put his thoughts in order.

Love. Nicole had used the word *love* to talk about Mathias, but Pascal had been in love before, and it hadn't felt like this. He and Robert had their ups and downs, of course, but he'd never questioned whether they belonged together or whether they could make things work between them. He'd questioned whether Robert could beat the cancer that had eventually killed him, and he'd questioned how he was supposed to go on without his lover, but never if they were right for each other.

With Mathias he couldn't stop asking that question. He took a deep breath and washed his hands before he returned to the restaurant floor. He still didn't know what he was going to tell his ladies, but he couldn't delay any longer without taking an official break.

Their cosmos were ready at the bar, so he loaded those onto the tray and carried them to the table. "I told Nick to make up a pitcher so he'd have them ready when you wanted more," he teased as he set the glasses in front of each of them.

"You could just bring the pitcher to the table," Hélène replied. "But bring a glass for yourself if you do that."

Pascal laughed. "What did you decide on for dinner?"

They ordered quickly, and he went to place the order with the kitchen. As he came back out, the display martini glass that would easily hold three or four liters of liquid caught his eye. He snagged it as he passed and headed back to the table. "I brought a glass," he said as he sank into the chair Camille had pushed out for him earlier.

His ladies erupted into gales of laughter, and just like that, the tension beneath his lungs evaporated. He couldn't sit there with them, surrounded by laughter, and not feel buoyed by it.

All four of them lifted their glasses to clink against the one in his hand. "What are we drinking to?" Martine asked.

"Or what are we drinking to forget?" Camille added.

"Things with Mathias have gotten… complicated."

"Why is that?" Nicole asked.

Pascal shrugged. "We're just so different."

"You'll never be bored," Martine quipped. Pascal grimaced. "Joking aside, opposites attract is a staple in romance for a reason, you know."

"Maybe, but reality isn't as simple as your books."

"How are you different?" Nicole inquired. "The important ways, not things like he has blond hair and you have black."

He knew where she stood on the matter of differences in a relationship. Even if he hadn't known about her husband, her books almost always featured couples from different cultures.

"I wasn't going to list that. I do have some sense." He took a deep breath and tried to decide where to start. "I don't think we want the same things."

"At all, or is there something particular that's bothering you?" Camille said.

Pascal tried to put into words the sense of unease that hadn't completely left him since he'd woken up with Mathias still in his bed the day before. "I remember what it was like to be twentysomething, when all it took was the first hint of interest and I was raring to go."

"You say that like it's a bad thing," Hélène teased. Pascal wasn't surprised the comment came from her. While Hélène's books always resolved romantically, it wasn't unusual for her characters to start their relationships on a purely sexual level before developing deeper feelings for each other.

"It wasn't when I was in my twenties and with Robert and we both wanted the same thing," Pascal agreed.

"What does he want that you don't?" Martine said.

Sex, Pascal almost said, but that wasn't true. He wanted to have sex with Mathias. He had just wanted to wait for their relationship to support it. "I don't know, but it always feels like he's ten steps ahead of me, rushing into everything, rushing into a relationship, rushing into bed, just rushing."

"He is young. That's pretty normal, I'd think. How long did it take you and Robert to fall into bed?" Nicole said.

Pascal shrugged. "I don't remember. Probably not as long as it should have."

"Why should it have taken longer?" Nicole asked. "If you loved each other—and you obviously did—why would waiting have made a difference?"

"Because I'm not sure I knew I loved him when it happened," Pascal replied. "And no, I'm not such a prude that I think you should only have sex with people you love, but I'm not a big fan of sex for the sake of sex either."

"How does Mathias feel about it?"

He looked away, unable to keep Nicole's gaze with the weight of that question hanging in the air. "You haven't seen the way he flirts at the bar."

"I've seen the way you flirt here," Martine said. "You flirt with us the entire time we're here. You've never taken any of *us* home with you."

"That's because I'm gay and you're married."

"Not the point. Just because he flirts to keep the customers happy and make better tips doesn't mean he's sleeping around or even that he wants to sleep around. Give him a little credit."

"I'm trying, but I've already had my great love story. I had my soul mate. Isn't that what you call them in your books? The one fated person you were meant to love above all others."

Camille, seated closest to him, patted his hand. "Soul mates are made, not fated."

"And a second chance at love is the second oldest cliché in the book," Hélène added.

"What's the oldest?"

"Love at first sight," they said in unison.

He laughed. "I dodged that one, at least." He stood up. "I need to check on your appetizers and my other tables. I'll think about what you said, though, and I'll be back in a little bit."

"Pascal," Hélène said as he started away. He turned back to look at her. "Did you have sex with Mathias?"

He nodded.

"Did you *want* to have sex with him?"

He smirked at her. "What kind of question is that?"

"Okay, let me phrase it this way. Did you intend to have sex with him when you did?"

That drew him up short. "No, I didn't."

"Is that what's bothering you?"

"I don't want it to mean less to him than it did to me," he said so softly he wasn't sure they could hear him.

"Then maybe you should tell him that."

Pascal nodded to show that he'd heard her, but he couldn't answer, not with the realization surging through him of what he'd just said and all that it implied. He went through the mechanics of serving their appetizers, bringing the bill for his early table, and checking everything in the back to make sure all was running smoothly, not that he'd have noticed anything short of a grease fire. His mind was reeling, and he couldn't seem to pull himself back together. Despite all his worries and fears, he'd started falling for Mathias, which only made his fears worse. If things didn't work out, if Mathias left him…. He pushed the thought aside. He'd promised Benjamin he wouldn't doom their relationship before it had a chance to start. He could do this. He could talk to Mathias on Saturday like an adult, and they could work things out. If it turned out they didn't want the same things, he'd deal with it somehow. And if it turned out they did want the same things, maybe he could finally stop feeling like Damocles waiting for the sword to fall.

CHAPTER 14

MATHIAS ROLLED out of bed groggily on Saturday morning. He and Pascal had exchanged a few more texts since Wednesday's invitation to go biking, enough to establish that they both had late nights on Friday and that they shouldn't try to wake up early to go out. They'd agreed to meet at one and go from there. His clock informed him it was eleven fifteen, which gave him plenty of time to take a shower and get ready to meet Pascal. He pushed open the drapes to see what the weather was like, only to be greeted by curtains of rain in the generously labeled "courtyard" outside his apartment. So much for biking. He reached for his phone to text Pascal about what they should do instead, but he changed his mind halfway through typing the message. He hated the hesitations he couldn't get rid of, but he'd made such a mistake the last time he tried to take the initiative with Pascal that he felt paralyzed now. He set the phone back down and went into the bathroom. Whatever they ended up doing, he needed a shower before they did it. He could do that and hope Pascal had texted him by the time he finished.

He ran through the things he needed to say to Pascal in his mind as he turned the water to hot and waited for it to warm up enough to flip the water flow from the tub to the shower nozzle. He needed to apologize, first and foremost, to make sure Pascal understood he wouldn't make the same mistake of taking silence for consent again. Then he needed to make sure Pascal had enjoyed it, even if he didn't want to do it again anytime soon. And then he needed to see where that left them. He'd understand if Pascal was done with him, although hopefully his suggestion of doing something besides just talking meant that he wasn't ready to kick Mathias to the curb just yet. What would be the point of planning to bike through the park if he intended to break up with Mathias? Of course that wasn't a guarantee, but he clung to the hope as he shampooed his hair and washed away the smell of sweat and alcohol that lingered from his shift last night.

It had been insanely busy, which was good for tips, but he'd had more than the usual number of handsy customers, and that left him feeling doubly dirty. He wouldn't have minded if those hands had belonged to Pascal, but he'd had enough of strangers groping his ass. He'd still wear the tight jeans and the shirts that rode up to expose a hint of skin, and he'd still smile at them, one step short of inviting, because that's what was expected in a place like Le Salon, but the little thrill he'd gotten when he first started at the thought that he was attractive enough for someone to want to grope him had long since worn off.

If Pascal wanted to grope him, on the other hand....

Mathias stopped that thought before he could complete it. He'd already pushed the limits of acceptable behavior with Pascal once. He wouldn't do it again. He'd wait for Pascal to bring it up if it killed him.

He shut the water off and reached for his towel, refusing to dwell on the memories of how good it had felt to have Pascal's hands on him. It didn't matter how good they'd felt. He'd have to do without.

When he was dressed, he picked up his phone to check out of habit, not that he expected to have a message from Pascal yet. It wasn't even noon, and they weren't supposed to meet until one. To his surprise, Pascal's name appeared at the top of his text record.

No biking today, I'm afraid. Come upstairs whenever you're ready. We can have lunch and talk.

Whenever you're ready.... Mathias wasn't sure he'd ever be ready, but that was a different problem.

I have to shower and get dressed. I'll be up in about half an hour. That would give him a little more time to get his thoughts together and wouldn't make him seem too eager to see Pascal. The thought hurt, because a week ago, he'd have jumped at the chance for a little more time, but he'd blown that when he couldn't keep it in his pants.

Take your time. I'll be here.

Mathias set his phone aside and paced the length of his bedroom. He'd bought himself time, but now he had to fill it. He could eat, but Pascal had mentioned lunch. If he ate something now, he wouldn't be hungry for lunch. He didn't know what Pascal had planned since they had talked about going biking, not having lunch, but even so, it would be rude to refuse.

He ran his hand through his hair and wondered if he should style it. He'd have to do it before he went to Le Salon that night. It would save time later if he did it now, but he'd come from the bar on Tuesday, all tight clothes, spiked hair, and out-of-control libido. Maybe it would be better to stay as far from that persona as possible for the next while, certainly until he knew where he stood with Pascal.

He went into the kitchen to make a cup of coffee. That would help pass the time, and the caffeine would wake him up more. He was already jittery, but he didn't figure it could get any worse, caffeine or no caffeine. When the coffee was ready, he made himself sit at the table and sip at it until half an hour had passed.

He set the cup in the sink to deal with later, pulled on a pair of shoes, took a deep breath, and headed upstairs. His pulse pounded in his ears as he knocked on Pascal's door and waited. He stuck his hands into his pockets, trying for nonchalant, although with his luck, it made him look like a kid. He certainly felt like one.

Pascal answered the door promptly, looking as put together as ever in a simple long-sleeved shirt and gray slacks. Mathias bit his lip, a reminder to himself to stay in control.

"Come in. How was work last night?"

"Busy," Mathias said. "Not that I'm complaining. I make more money that way." He stepped inside so Pascal could close the door behind him. "What about you?"

"Thursday was slow because of the weather, but we had a crowd last night. I didn't get home until after one." Pascal gestured for Mathias to precede him into the living room. Mathias took a seat in the armchair, not sure Pascal would want to sit next to him on the couch. The tension in the room built until Mathias couldn't stand it anymore.

"I'm sorry about Tuesday night," he blurted out. "I was out of line. I didn't even give you a chance to say no." It wasn't the most elegant apology he could have given, but at least it got everything out in the open.

Pascal looked surprised at that. "I seem to remember your ass in the air, not the other way around. You hardly forced me into fucking you."

Mathias's cheeks burned at the blunt words, his skin too tight over bone. He remembered all too clearly how it had felt to have Pascal behind him, reaming him until he couldn't breathe with it. He shifted on the cushion. "Maybe not, but I didn't exactly ask before I started pulling your clothes off either."

Pascal shrugged. "What's done is done. We had sex. It happens."

Mathias's stomach sank. He hadn't imagined the conversation would be easy, but he'd hoped for... something besides this casual indifference. "What happens now?"

Pascal sighed and ran his hand through his hair, messing it up in a way Mathias would have found irresistible in any other circumstances. "I don't know. That's why you're here. So we can figure it out. At least I hope that's why you're here."

"Yes, of course." Relief surged through Mathias, speeding his pulse and stealing his breath. Pascal might not have answers, but he wasn't ending things either. "I wasn't sure if you'd still want that. After I...."

"After you barged in with sex on your mind when you knew I wasn't ready for that to be on the table," Pascal finished. He held up his hand when Mathias started to apologize again. "You didn't force me into anything. I could have stopped you and I didn't. That's not the issue."

"But there is an issue," Mathias said. "If there weren't, you wouldn't have been so strange the next morning or when we talked."

Pascal huffed a bitter laugh. "There are too many issues to count. I don't even know where to start. Don't apologize again. All you did was bring things to a head faster. They would have been issues anyway."

That didn't sound promising. Mathias sank back into the chair, feeling the gulf between them growing with each passing second. "Do you want me to leave?"

"Do you want to leave?" Pascal countered.

Mathias shook his head, but Pascal continued to look at him expectantly, so he tried to put his thoughts in some semblance of order. "Meeting you was a stroke of luck I never believed I'd get." He took a deep breath as he debated what to say next. "I work at a bank during the day where the chances of personal interaction are few. At night I work in a bar where I flirt with customers because that's how I get tips. It's business, nothing more. I figured I wouldn't get a chance for more than that until the training period at the bank was over and I got enough of a raise to be able to quit working at the bar. Then I could go out and actually try to meet people I might be interested in. Then you came in, and all those plans went right out the window, except why would you be interested in me? I'm just a kid, and you're...."

"I'm what?" Pascal asked.

"Fishing for compliments?" Mathias teased, but the joke fell flat. He sighed. "You're everything I'm not. You're put together. You know what you want in life. You have a career already. You have a great apartment. You don't worry about whether you can achieve everything you set out to do because you've already achieved it."

"Is that really how you see me?" Pascal asked.

"Of course it is. How else would I see you?"

Pascal snorted. "An old man desperate to reclaim his youth by hooking up with someone half his age? A waiter who never amounted to anything of worth in his life? A fool who's afraid to get in too deep in a new relationship because the only one he's had that ever mattered ended far too soon? There's no shortage of other ways, and none of them are good."

Mathias stared at Pascal as his brain raced to process the words that spewed from him. The pain beneath the surface scored him deeply. He wanted to do something, anything to take that look off Pascal's face, but he didn't know if he'd be welcome. "I don't see you that way," he said finally, because he had to say something.

"That's something, I suppose, but it's what you'll hear about us. I'll always be older than you. You'll be this big-shot bank executive, and I'll still be just a waiter. You may not see me that way now, but how long will that last?" Pascal asked bitterly.

"If I have ever said or done anything to make you think I feel that way or even that I care about things like that, I'm sorry," Mathias said slowly. He couldn't remember anything specific he might have said or done, but not realizing Pascal harbored those doubts, he hadn't been careful to avoid the topics either. "I know I act without thinking sometimes, but I never meant to make you feel that way."

"I was married once, or the closest thing to it," Pascal said. Mathias blinked at the sudden change of topic, but he was willing to follow along. "We didn't call it marriage then. It hadn't been legalized in Québec yet, but we'd promised each other a lifetime together."

"What happened?" Mathias asked, not entirely sure he wanted to know. Pascal obviously lived alone now, but that didn't explain how he'd ended up that way.

"He died."

Mathias flinched. Québec had legalized gay marriage in 2004. If they had been the same age, Pascal's partner would have been in his early thirties when he died. Mathias had been a child, but he knew the history of the AIDS epidemic and how many thousands of men had died in the nineties before the current medical cocktails were discovered. Had Pascal's partner been one of those deaths? Was that why he was so particular about sex? "I'm sorry to hear that."

"Robert had bone tumors. We tried everything the doctors could think of, but we found them too late," Pascal said. "He was my world, and then he was gone. I never believed I'd get a second chance."

Mathias couldn't stand it. He pushed out of his seat and reached for Pascal. Pascal pulled back reflexively, but before Mathias could lower his arms and slink away, Pascal stepped into the embrace. Mathias rested his arms on Pascal's hips and leaned against him. He didn't know what comfort his presence would offer, but he would stand there as long as Pascal wanted. He wouldn't pull away first.

He knew the hug didn't solve anything, but it felt good. He hoped it felt the same to Pascal, tangible proof that Mathias was still there and intended to still be there if Pascal would have him.

CHAPTER 15

PASCAL LEANED into Mathias's arms. When was the last time he'd let someone comfort him? He'd had to be the strong one when Robert was sick. He'd been the strong one each time they lost a friend. He'd been the rock everyone else leaned on, even when he was shattering inside. To have Mathias see through that façade was unexpected but not unwelcome. Not unwelcome at all.

He breathed in the scent of Mathias's aftershave and let it soothe his frayed nerves. He'd known the conversation would be tense, although he hadn't seen Mathias's primary concern coming. At least he could resolve one thing between them, even if the rest was still a tangled mess of issues and emotions. As good as it felt to stand there, they wouldn't solve anything with a hug.

He lifted his head and summoned a smile for Mathias. It felt brittle on his face, but it was an improvement over frowning. "Are you hungry? I promised you lunch."

Mathias looked surprised at the comment. Pascal squeezed his waist. "We can talk more after we eat, but I think we both need a break."

Mathias still looked like he wanted to barge on with the conversation, but he followed Pascal into the tiny kitchen and helped him carry bowls and a tureen of soup out to the table. "I didn't know people still had things like that," he said, pointing to the soup container.

"It was my grandmother's," Pascal said. "She gave her good china to my sister, but Sylvie never used it. She gave it to me a couple of years after Mamie died. I don't have a lot of call for good china, but I think she'd like it that I use it, even if it's not for fancy parties."

Pascal ladled up the squash potage into the bowls and put the lid back on the tureen.

Mathias took a taste of the soup and smiled broadly. "This is really good."

"Don't sound so surprised," Pascal teased, striving for normalcy. "I know how to cook."

Mathias laughed. "Then you're better off than I am. I don't go hungry, but it never tastes this good."

Pascal almost offered to teach him, but that assumed a future together, and he wasn't sure that was still on the table. Mathias hadn't gone running when Pascal let loose the vitriol that had been building up inside him, but that hardly meant he was willing to stay around long-term. He took a spoonful of the soup and tried to think of something to pass the time while they ate. They'd have to talk more after they were done, but he wanted the meal to be an oasis of peace before they started again.

"When's your next training at the bank?" Interest in Mathias's career was a safe topic.

"Next month," Mathias replied. "Then I'm done with training weekends for a while. I'll have some more to do next year sometime, I think. I don't have the whole two-year program memorized."

"That's good," Pascal said. "You need a break. If nothing else, you'll be able to sleep in on Saturdays and Sundays now."

"Or spend them with you," Mathias said.

Pascal looked down at his suddenly fascinating soup. Maybe talking about Mathias's future wasn't such a good way to avoid talking about *their* future.

"If that's something you still want to do." Mathias's voice sounded so small that Pascal looked back up sharply.

"I still have to spend some Sundays with my parents." Pascal felt like a complete bastard when Mathias's face fell even more. "Finish your lunch. We'll figure things out."

Mathias nodded and went back to his soup, but Pascal could feel the gulf growing between them with each passing moment spent in silence. Mathias finished the bowl and looked expectantly at Pascal, who hadn't managed more than two or three mouthfuls. With a stifled sigh, he carried the tureen back into the kitchen and returned to where Mathias waited.

He sat this time, though he didn't know how long he'd stay seated. Mathias took the spot on the couch next to him. Pascal took a deep breath and faced Mathias. "What do you want out of this?" He gestured between them.

"Whatever you're willing to give me," Mathias replied.

Pascal shook his head. "That's not actually helpful, and it's not what I asked. What do *you* want?"

"Everything you'll let me have," Mathias said, "and before you tell me that's not helpful either, think about it from my perspective. If I tell you I want forever and you're looking for a fling, where does that leave me?"

"You already know I don't want a fling," Pascal pointed out.

"But I don't really know what you do want," Mathias said. "You haven't given me anything to go on. I know you look at me and see a kid, and next to you, I am a kid. I get that. But don't dismiss me just because I'm young. I worked damn hard to get where I am, and I'm working even harder to stay here. I'm not some rich kid playing at having a job. I'm from rural Québec. My parents barely speak English. My dad works in the paper mills, and my mother never worked. I grew up poor, the oldest kid, expected to work as soon as I was old enough. And maybe that makes me beneath you, just like waiting tables in a bar does, but that's not all I am or all I'll ever be."

"I know that," Pascal hurried to answer. "I don't know anyone who works harder than you."

"But you don't believe I'll work that hard at making things work between us."

Pascal wanted to refute that, but he wouldn't lie to Mathias. He'd fallen into exactly that trap. "It's not that so much as I'm having a hard time believing you'll want to put that much work into *me*. I look at you and see someone with so much potential, someone who's going somewhere. You don't want to be bogged down with me."

"How about you do us both a favor and stop assuming what I want or don't want?" Mathias suggested. "Because I don't see you the way you clearly see yourself, so I'm not thinking that way. You can't possibly think I don't want you after Tuesday night."

"You were horny and I was available."

"You're half-right, anyway," Mathias said. "I was horny. You have that effect on me. But you make it sound like you were the easiest or only option. You weren't. Even as dead as the bar was on Tuesday, I could have found someone to go home with if I'd wanted. Or I could have gone cruising in another bar. I didn't. I came here because you were here, and I didn't want a random fuck. I wanted you. That was a bit presumptuous on my part, since you'd made your position clear on the matter, but that didn't change how I felt about you."

Pascal couldn't stop the thrill that went through him at Mathias's words, because he knew how easily Mathias could have found someone else. "We should probably talk about that presumption bit."

Mathias sighed. "I'm sorry. I said it already, but I'll say it again, as often as you need me to."

"It's not the sex, per se, that bothers me," Pascal replied. "It's that you knew where I stood and you barged ahead anyway. It makes it hard to feel like my opinion on things matters to you."

Mathias slumped against the back of the couch. "I didn't think things through. I'm sorry. You should have stopped me."

"I should have," Pascal agreed, "but what's done is done. Sex changes things in a relationship, and I wasn't ready for that because I wasn't sure it meant as much to you as it does to me."

"Are you saying we can have sex now?" Mathias asked.

Pascal laughed. "Maybe not right this minute, but it's pointless to close the barn door after the horse has already escaped. We can't undo what we did. We can only decide how to move forward. If you really meant it when you said you were serious about making this work, then I have to take you at your word. And if I do that, then my reasons for waiting to have sex are no longer valid. But, Mathias…." He waited for Mathias to look up at him. "If I make my stance on something clear again, take that seriously. If I can't trust you, the rest doesn't matter."

Mathias looked so miserable that Pascal nearly regretted his words, but this was important. They had to be able to trust one another, and Mathias's actions had been a direct violation of that.

"You can trust me," Mathias said finally. "It won't happen again."

Pascal smiled even as he hoped Mathias was right. He reached across the space between them and closed his fingers around Mathias's. Mathias turned his hand so he could twine their fingers together. "Can we call in sick tonight and just stay right here instead?" Mathias asked.

Pascal chuckled. "I'm sure we could, but I'm not sure either of our budgets would appreciate it." Pascal could have afforded a night off, but Mathias couldn't, and he didn't want to rub that in.

"Don't remind me. Six more months. I can handle six more months of this."

"What happens in six months?" Pascal asked.

"I get a pay increase," Mathias said. "Not a large one, but enough that I can probably cut back to just working weekends at Le Salon."

Another six months at least of juggling nights off and crazy weekend schedules. He was too old for this, but if Mathias was willing to meet him halfway, Pascal wouldn't back out now. He switched Mathias's hand to his other one so he could stretch his arm around Mathias's shoulders. Mathias scooted closer and rested his head against Pascal. "When I was so afraid I'd screwed things up beyond repair, this is what I realized I'd miss the most," Mathias said in a soft voice.

"What?"

"Being with you like this. No demands, no pressure, no masks to wear for work or for play. Just being together. As amazing as the sex was—did I tell you it was really amazing?" Pascal nodded. It had been damn good sex. "Anyway, as amazing as the sex was, that wasn't what I would've missed the most."

Pascal pressed a kiss to the top of Mathias's head, the only part he could reach easily. Mathias tipped his head up to meet Pascal's lips with his own. Pascal kissed him again and shifted a little to get more comfortable.

"That doesn't mean I'd turn down a repeat of the sex either," Mathias added. "If you meant what you said about it being okay now."

Pascal glanced at the clock. They had time before he had to work, but he didn't want to rush the next time they had sex. He wanted to make love to Mathias properly. "I meant it, but not today. Some evening when we have time to relax and enjoy it instead of worrying that we'll have to hurry so we can get ready for work."

"You have an overinflated opinion of my stamina," Mathias said.

"Or you have an underinflated opinion of mine," Pascal purred in reply. Mathias shivered in his arms, much to Pascal's delight. Something good would come of his age. He nuzzled Mathias's cheek as he shifted on the couch again so Mathias rested against the back of the couch with Pascal leaning over him. Mathias lifted his chin, asking for a kiss, but Pascal avoided his mouth, preferring to draw this out. They had rushed the foreplay on Tuesday. Pascal intended to show Mathias the rewards of patience now. Mathias's skin felt like satin beneath his lips, soft and smooth with the hint of shaving cream to entice Pascal's nose. He brushed his lips over one high cheekbone while caressing Mathias's palm with his thumb.

Mathias caught his lower lip between his teeth, drawing Pascal's attention to his full, pouting mouth. He traced the abused flesh with one finger, holding Mathias's gaze with his own as he did. Mathias's face projected only innocent enthusiasm, but the way he sucked Pascal's finger into his mouth was anything but innocent. Pascal inhaled sharply, transfixed by Mathias's expression as he teased him. He didn't know what he'd done to be so lucky, but the very idea that this young, vibrant, gorgeous man wanted to be with him knocked the breath he'd managed to draw in from his lungs and left him dizzy with delight and need. He lowered his head to nuzzle at Mathias's jaw. Mathias tipped his head back, offering Pascal unrestricted access to his neck. Then he nipped at the tip of Pascal's finger.

"Brat," Pascal muttered against Mathias's skin. Mathias just did it again.

In retaliation, Pascal nipped at Mathias's pulse point.

"Yes," Mathias said through a hiss of breath. "Leave a mark. Let everyone who sees me at the bar tonight know I'm taken."

"And if it's still there on Monday when you have to go to the bank?" Pascal asked.

Mathias shrugged. "Then they'll know I'm taken too."

He shouldn't do it. Adrien wouldn't care at Le Salon, but if Mathias went to the bank on Monday with his neck covered in hickeys, his boss there could very well say something about his unprofessional appearance. He shouldn't do it, but even as he told himself that, he sank his teeth into the tender skin and sucked hard. Mathias's breath stuttered, and a soft groan escaped. Pascal started to lift his head to check Mathias's reaction, but Mathias held him in place. "More."

That answered that question. Pascal tipped Mathias backward on the couch and latched on again, a little lower this time, closer to the collar of his T-shirt, where it would be covered by the dress shirt he would wear to the bank. He bit down again, not hard enough to break skin, but more than enough to draw another gasp and moan from Mathias.

He worked his way even lower until he encountered the collar of Mathias's shirt. He pulled it aside and bit the curve of his shoulder. Mathias's entire body shuddered beneath him. "I'll have to remember that," Pascal murmured against Mathias's skin, his voice ripe with promise.

Mathias reached for the hem of his shirt, but Pascal caught his hand and lifted it to his lips. "I'll remember. We don't have to do everything today."

He turned Mathias's hand in his and nibbled on the inside of his wrist. Mathias bucked beneath him with a sharp gasp. "How the hell do you turn every patch of skin you touch into a direct line to my dick?"

Pascal grinned at him. "Talent."

Mathias smirked at him. "You'll have to teach me sometime."

Pascal smirked back, more than a little pleased with Mathias's reaction. "It will be my pleasure."

CHAPTER 16

MATHIAS PULLED off his hoodie and hung it up in the back room of Le Salon. He brushed absently over his T-shirt to make sure it wasn't wrinkled and headed out to the bar to check in with Michel about any specials for the night or any other menu changes. Adrien kept the bar well-stocked, but occasionally they would run out of something on the weekends when it was harder to get deliveries.

Michel looked him over slyly, gaze landing on Mathias's neck and the row of bruises an inch above his collar. "Those are new."

Mathias grinned. "Someone was feeling possessive this afternoon."

"Someone?"

"Pascal," Mathias said. "I wasn't complaining."

"Does Adrien know you're picking up his customers?" Michel asked.

"I'm not." Adrien had made his stance on that clear from the beginning. "We live in the same building. We ran into each other there. I mean, I see him when he comes in, obviously, but we've been dating for a while."

"Really? Rumor has it he's allergic to relationships," Michel replied.

Mathias shrugged. Rumor wasn't entirely wrong, but Mathias wasn't going to add fuel to that fire, not when he needed more than ever to prove he was worthy of Pascal's trust. Pascal wouldn't come in tonight, but he was a regular, to the point that the staff knew him by name. The next time he came in, he'd hear whatever Mathias said now. "Anything I need to know about the menu tonight?"

"No specials, nothing out of stock at the moment, so just do your thing and let someone know if you have any problems."

Michel had said that often the first few weeks Mathias had worked at the bar, but he hadn't felt the need in months. Had something changed? "Should I expect any?"

"Maybe," Michel said. "Some people will see those hickeys and figure you're taken. Others may see them and think it means you're easy."

"I know how to say no, and people here are good about listening."

"Let someone know if they don't," Michel repeated.

Adrien had given Mathias much the same talk when he hired him: be fun, be flirty, but don't let the patrons cross the line. The bouncers weren't just there to protect the customers. They would help the staff too. "I'll be careful," he said when he realized Michel was waiting for a reply.

"You'd better. Adrien would be upset if Pascal stopped coming in because his boyfriend got hurt on the job."

Mathias grinned. Boyfriend. He loved the sound of that. He was Pascal's boyfriend, and the marks on his neck proclaimed that to anyone who cared to notice. He turned out onto the floor to wipe tables and make himself useful until he had customers in his section. When they got busy—and on a Saturday, they'd be busy before long—everyone helped out where needed instead of staying in one section, but he wouldn't barge in on someone else until it got crowded.

He nodded to the other waiters as he worked, catching a few glances at his neck. He smiled back smugly. He didn't know that much about any of their personal lives, but he'd put money on none of them having a man like Pascal to go home to. They might not all see him as the catch he was—Pascal didn't see himself that way—but Mathias knew how lucky he was to have caught Pascal's eye. He'd have to keep saying it until Pascal believed him. Or even better, he'd have to seduce him every chance he got. That ought to take care of any idea in Pascal's head that he was unattractive in Mathias's eyes. It probably went deeper than sex appeal, but Mathias could start there. As outrageously good as Pascal had made him feel that afternoon with a few kisses and over-the-clothes caresses, Mathias was already looking forward to what would happen the next time they had time to lose the clothes. Not that he knew exactly when that would be, but he'd find a time. He didn't have training next weekend, and Pascal's sister would be the one to visit their parents. They'd both have to work at night, but they could spend all morning and early afternoon in bed both days if Pascal was amenable. Mathias would have to convince him to be amenable.

Mathias adjusted the fit of his jock as that train of thought had a predictable effect. The jock provided a layer of cloth between his cock and his jeans but little else. He'd have to watch his thoughts, or he'd be serving tables with a boner to go along with his hickeys. That thought made him grin. Pascal had done a number on him, and he couldn't be happier about it.

"You look like you had a good night."

"You could say that," Mathias replied with a grin for Graham, the only server at Le Salon newer than he was.

"Lucky you."

"Don't I know it."

A group of men came in before Graham could say anything else and took a seat at one of Mathias's tables. "Work calls. Talk to you later." He checked to make sure he had a pad to take orders and headed toward the table of men he didn't recognize. That wasn't unusual, especially on a Saturday night, but he always enjoyed seeing the regulars.

"Hello, bonjour," he said. "I'm Mathias. I'll be taking care of you tonight. What can I get you to drink?"

The men looked up at his words. Three of them smiled easily, but the fourth gave him a more careful once-over. Mathias kept his smile fixed but didn't add the extra warmth in his voice. Michel's warning held him back. He didn't want trouble.

"What's good?" Trouble asked.

"Our bartender is excellent," Mathias replied. "I'm sure he can make any drink you order to your satisfaction. If you're looking for a suggestion, though, his new pear martini has been very popular."

"That sounds good," one of Trouble's friends said. "I'll have one of those."

The other two nodded. Mathias looked back at Trouble. "Make it a round?" he asked.

Trouble leaned a little closer. Mathias didn't take a step back, tempted as he was, but he'd make sure to stand on the opposite side of the table when he came back with their drinks. "If a cute thing like you recommends it, I'm sure it's good."

Mathias barely refrained from snorting at the lame come-on. Pascal was so much smoother than this loser.

"I'll be back with your drinks." He headed toward the bar to place the order with Michel.

Something must have shown in his expression, because Michel asked, "Everything okay?"

"It's fine," Mathias said. "One of the guys at my table thinks he's suave. He's a joke. Nothing I can't handle."

"Remember what I said earlier. If you can handle him, great. But don't feel like you have to handle him on your own," Michel reminded him.

An hour ago Mathias had brushed off the reminder. Now, he was glad of the security it offered. He didn't think Trouble would be more than an annoyance, but it was reassuring to know he didn't have to deal with it if it went beyond that. He checked to see if he had any other tables yet, but it was still early. After Michel had fixed the drinks, Mathias loaded his tray and returned to the table, careful to stand across from Trouble rather than next to him. No reason to make it easy for him to get a grope in.

"Here you go, gentlemen," he said as he passed the drinks around. "Pear martinis." He waited as they sipped before asking, "What do you think?"

"Delicious," Trouble said, raking his gaze the length of Mathias's body. The other three echoed the approval without the leers. Mathias took that as his excuse to escape. He'd dealt with slimy customers before. Why did Trouble make him feel so much dirtier than the others had?

He retreated to the bar, well out of Trouble's reach, while he waited for his other tables to fill or for someone else to need a hand. It didn't take long before he had a new set of customers... right by Trouble's table. He studied the layout of the space for a moment, trying to find a place to stand that would let him talk to his new customers while staying out of Trouble's reach. He didn't know for sure the man would grope him, but given the way he'd been watching Mathias, it seemed likely. Unfortunately he couldn't see a way to do it without being obvious. He'd have to hope Trouble behaved himself.

He was halfway through taking the orders at the second table when he felt the surreptitious grope. He shifted enough to dislodge the unwelcome touch and braced for a confrontation if it returned, but he was able to finish their order in peace. When he was done with them, he edged around Trouble's table to the opposite side again before checking if they needed anything. Trouble looked like he was about to say something, but his friends waved Mathias off before he could.

Mathias returned to the bar with the second order. "Did he cop a feel?" Michel asked as Mathias waited for the drinks.

"Yeah. Hardly the first time it's happened. Probably won't be the last either. I don't like it, but it's not worth making a scene over. Not unless he goes further than a harmless grope."

"That's a slippery slope," Michel warned. "Watch yourself."

"I will," Mathias promised.

He dropped the drinks off at his second table and escaped without Trouble grabbing him again. He checked the rest of his area and smiled when he recognized Pascal's friends. "René and Benjamin, right?" he said as he approached the table. "How are you tonight?"

"Doing well. How about you?" one of them—René, Mathias thought—asked.

"Bracing for a busy night," Mathias said, "but other than that, I'm great."

René gave Mathias's neck a speculative look. "I'd say Pascal agrees."

Mathias flushed even as he grinned. He didn't know how much they knew about the problems of the past week, but odds were good Pascal had told them at least a little. "He didn't kick me out, so I'd say you're right."

"You do understand what a big step this is for him, don't you?" Benjamin asked.

Mathias nodded. "He told me about Robert. I guess you knew him too?"

"Yes, we both did. He and Pascal were everything to each other for the years they had together, but that was a long time ago."

"Is that supposed to make me feel better or worse?" Mathias asked, not quite joking.

"Neither." Benjamin caught his gaze and held it, his face serious. "Pascal will measure your relationship against those memories if you let him. You can't let him because you can't win. He won't be happy at forty-eight the way he was at twenty-eight. It's not the way we're wired as human beings. It's not a question of better or worse. Just keep him grounded in the present instead of letting him get lost in the past."

"He likes to top," René added. "What he really needs, though, is someone who isn't afraid to top him too."

"René," Benjamin said with a huff. "You can't go around saying things like that."

"Why not? It's true and you know it."

Benjamin looked back at Mathias. "I'll have a Bellini, please. Don't listen to René. He thrives on being outrageous."

"Is he wrong?" Mathias asked.

"That's a question you'd have to ask Pascal. We've been friends most of our lives. We were never lovers."

Mathias had wondered but hadn't wanted to ask. It wasn't any of his business as long as it was in the past, even if they had been. He focused back on his job. It was safer than thinking about Pascal. "What would you like, René?"

"One of those spicy margaritas you made for me the night we met you," René said.

"The chipotle margarita?"

"Yeah, that one."

"Coming right up."

By the time he returned with their drinks, the bar was too busy for him to stay and chat. Then again, they hadn't come in to visit with him anyway. He kept moving constantly until it was time for his break around ten. "Watch the table of four over there," he warned Graham. "The guy with his back to us is handsy."

"Aren't they all?" Graham said with a shake of his head.

Mathias shrugged before walking toward the break room. He slumped down into the chair and took a deep breath as he considered Graham's comment. Was Trouble really worse than any of the hundred men who'd groped him at one time or another since he'd started working at Le Salon? Or was the difference in his own perception of the situation?

When he'd first started working at the bar, the attention of the customers had been a huge ego boost. He'd been the only gay boy in his admittedly small high school, although there'd been a couple of girls who were out as well. That had changed in college, but even then, he'd always felt like the odd man out. Here, though, he was the object of admiration from all directions, and he played into it for all he was worth. Tight shirts, tighter jeans, a bit of eyeliner, a swish in his walk, he'd done everything he could to draw their attention to his body, and he'd reveled in the rush of power every time one of them reached for him. It had felt *good* to be desired that way.

Then Pascal had looked right through him at the bar and right at him in his suit, and his world had tipped on its axis. To the men in the bar, his ass was his best feature. Pascal had been plenty appreciative once they finally got naked, but he'd been even more appreciative of Mathias's brain and his determination and his willingness to put in the hours at the bank to get ahead in his job.

Oh shit, he had it bad.

How was he supposed to go back out there—tonight or any night—and let men grope him now that he understood how much better it felt to be desired for who he was rather than how he looked? What had once gotten him worked up and eager to get home so he could jerk off now left him shying away because the hands on his ass weren't the ones he wanted. If Pascal decided to come grope him in the bar, Mathias would snuggle right down on his lap for the whole world to see, but no one else's touch was welcome.

He'd gotten good at the fun, flirty, inviting smile, and it had worked for him. Men responded to the fantasy he embodied and tipped him accordingly, especially when he didn't protest the occasional wandering hands. He'd have to unlearn all that now and see if he couldn't develop a professional, hands-off smile without costing himself so much in tips that he couldn't afford to keep his apartment. Even knowing those touches promised nothing, he shuddered at being the object of their fantasies now.

"You okay?"

Mathias looked up to see Adrien at the door.

"Yeah, just taking a break. One of the customers grabbed my ass, and it threw me off-balance."

"Which one? I'll see to them for the rest of the night."

"I can handle it," Mathias protested. "It just caught me off guard."

"You'll get your tip," Adrien said. "If it threw you this badly after all the months you've been working here, then it crossed a line."

Or else Mathias's line had moved.

Something of his thoughts must have shown on his face because Adrien patted his shoulder. "It's different when you have a boyfriend to go home to, isn't it?"

"Yeah. I didn't expect it to make a difference, or not this much of one. I mean, that's real. This is just business."

"No, it's not just business if it bothers you," Adrien said. "We're a bar, not a sex shop. I can't stop them from looking, but you have every right to stop them from touching, no matter where that line is for you. And if that line moves, that's fine. What constitutes sexual harassment is different for each person who works here. There's a reason Michel is behind the bar and not serving tables, and it's not just because he makes a mean drink. I don't step in unless I'm asked to because I can't judge where the line is for anyone but myself, but I will not have my employees harassed by customers. One table's worth of revenue won't bankrupt me."

"Thank you. It didn't bother me until tonight, but…."

"I had doubts when you started, but you've proven what a hard worker you are. The regulars like you because you pay attention to their preferences and remember them. I don't want to lose you now because something happens on the floor."

"Thanks, that really means a lot." Mathias looked down at his clothes. Maybe it was time to find a few pairs of jeans that weren't quite so tight. He could always wear the tight ones to entice Pascal.

"Which table?"

Adrien's words jolted Mathias out of that little fantasy. He cleared his throat to buy himself a second before replying. "Table sixteen."

"I'll handle them for the rest of the night. See me before you leave for your tip." He left before Mathias could thank him again. He slumped back in the chair and tried to figure out how this had become his life.

CHAPTER 17

PASCAL KNOCKED on the door on his parents' apartment precisely at noon on Sunday. He had a key, but he didn't feel right just barging in. His parents weren't as spry as they used to be, but they could still answer their own door.

"Pascal, come in. You know you don't have to knock." Pascal's father held the door wide so Pascal could come in. He leaned down and kissed the weathered cheek.

"Hello, Papa. How are you today?"

"The same as always," Papa replied. "Your mother is still primping, but we'll be ready for lunch soon. Where are you taking us today?"

"Where do you want to go? We can go back to the Italian restaurant you like so much, or we can try a new seafood restaurant that opened up in Ville-Marie near the Vieux Port."

"You know that area is overpriced and aimed at the tourists."

"I do, but I also know it's gotten very good reviews from people I trust, and the prices don't appear to be out of line with what they're offering. But if you want Italian, that's fine as well."

"Your mother will want to try the new place," Papa grumbled. "She always wants to try new places."

Pascal smiled at his father. Those two sentences summed up the entirety of his parents' fifty-plus years of marriage. "If it's not up to your standards, you can blame me after lunch. Does Maman have the grocery list ready? We can stop on the way home if you're not too tired after lunch."

"We're not invalids. We can go to the grocery with you like we do every week."

Papa's assertion wouldn't stop Pascal from offering to go without them. He might say they weren't invalids, but Pascal could see them growing more feeble as time passed. They'd celebrated his father's eightieth birthday earlier this year, and his mother wasn't far behind, and neither of them was in the best of health anymore. Even more concerning was his mother's tendency to get confused and not remember where she was or when things had happened. The last time he'd visited, she'd asked him where Robert was. He hoped she would be clearer today because he wanted to tell them about Mathias, and that would be easier done without her thinking Robert was still alive.

"Pascal, you're here early," Maman said as she came out of the bedroom. She had done her hair and makeup and looked as beautifully put together as ever. Her eyes were bright and alert, making him hopeful he would be able to tell them about Mathias over lunch.

"Maman, it's good to see you." He almost teased her about being late rather than him being early, but she would reply that a lady was never late. "I was telling Papa about a new seafood restaurant some friends recommended. Unless you'd rather have Italian?"

"You know I always want to try new places. How else will I know what my options are next time?"

Papa harrumphed next to them, but he offered his arm to Maman. Pascal held the door open for them and made sure it locked behind them before following them out to his car. He tried not to hover too obviously. At least it was only September still. In another month, his mother would have to replace her heels with boots.

They chatted about inconsequential things as they drove to the restaurant, Maman telling Pascal about the latest doings of her bridge club, and Papa grumbling about how they spent all their time drinking sherry and gossiping rather than actually playing. Pascal remembered those games from when he lived at home. He didn't know how things were now, but his mother's friends had been cutthroat players once upon a time, no matter how much sherry they drank or gossip they exchanged. He hoped time hadn't changed that.

When they had ordered and were enjoying their aperitifs, Pascal took a deep breath and tried to figure out how to tell his parents about Mathias.

"Maman, Papa, I met someone a few months ago."

"You meet people all the time," Maman said. "I love your stories from the restaurant. Who did you meet this time?"

"Hush, Marguerite, Pascal isn't talking about someone from the restaurant, are you, son?"

"No, Papa, I'm not. Mathias lives in my building. He works at the BMO."

"A banker. Very impressive," Maman said. "How did you meet?"

Pascal wondered what she would say if she knew they'd met at Le Salon. "He was leaving for work one morning as I came back from a run," Pascal said. "And then we ran into each other a couple of other times in the building and in the neighborhood. One thing led to another."

Maman reached across the table and patted his hand. "I know how much you loved Robert. We did too. He was our son just as much as you are. But you're too young to be alone for the rest of your life. I'm glad you've met someone. You should have brought him to lunch with you today."

"I wanted to talk to you first," Pascal said. "And things are... complicated. He's younger than I am, and I wasn't sure until recently that we wanted the same things out of a relationship." He still wasn't entirely sure, but he'd promised Mathias and himself that he wouldn't let those doubts control him.

"Pssh, age is just a number," Maman said. "And the best things in life are complicated. How did we not teach him that, Julien?"

Papa snorted. "We did. Then he lost Robert. It's hard to hold on to that when you've lost the love of your life after only ten years. Next time you come to lunch, bring him with you."

"Yes, Papa."

PASCAL LET himself back into his apartment after finishing the grocery shopping with his parents. They'd let him leave fairly quickly after that, amid calls for him to bring Mathias with him next time. He'd have to talk to Mathias and see if he'd be up for that. Meeting the parents was a big step, and they were still on shaky ground. He wouldn't push, but after talking with his parents, he needed to make the offer.

His phone beeped as he hung his jacket up in the closet. He pulled it from his pocket, hoping it would be Mathias. They probably wouldn't have time to see each other before Mathias had to go to the bar, but they could talk for a bit.

It was René. He didn't grimace like he wanted to. He could always call Mathias after he'd talked to René.

Your boy looked happy last night at the bar. Did you kiss and make up?

Pascal rolled his eyes and texted back. *If you saw him, you know we did.*

Pascal's phone rang almost immediately.

"Hello, René."

"You dog," René teased. "I haven't seen a collection of hickeys like that in a long time."

Pascal flushed. "He kept asking for more. I couldn't say no."

René snorted in amusement. "I repeat, you dog. Seriously, though, everything's good now?"

"It's better," Pascal replied, because if he couldn't be honest with René and Benjamin, who could he be honest with? René might be somewhere between irreverent and downright crude at times, but he'd stood by Pascal when he needed it most. "There's a lot to figure out, and it's stuff that isn't just going to go away because we talked about it—the age difference and all that entails, for starters. But we did talk about it, and we agreed to give it a go, a real go. No more dancing around each other, hoping the other one is as serious about it."

"I'm glad," René said. "You've been alone a long time. And I get that you needed the time to mourn before you could think about trying again. I can't even imagine what it would feel like to lose Benjamin. But you did that and moved on, except you didn't. Fifteen years is enough time."

"You're starting to sound like Benjamin. Is he rubbing off on you?"

"Not at the moment," René retorted. "He's gone for a walk."

Pascal rolled his eyes. *That* was more like it. "I'm trying. That's the best I can say right now. I really am trying, and so is he. The rest is a question of time and seeing how things work out."

"For what it's worth, he really did look happy last night, and not the put-on, 'let me flirt with everyone so I get a good tip' kind of happy that so many of the waiters have mastered. He looked genuinely happy."

That made Pascal smile. He knew all too well the façade waiters wore to improve the chances of a good tip. If his façade involved more sophistication and less sex appeal, it didn't make it less of a façade. He had mastered the polite, friendly smile that he gave to pretty much all his customers except his ladies. To know that he'd made Mathias happy enough for that to break through his usual "see how fuckable I am" routine was a huge stroke to Pascal's ego.

"Thanks for telling me. Go take a walk with Benjamin. I'm going to call Mathias before he has to go to work."

"Happy sexting."

Pascal hung up and called Mathias instead of replying.

"Hello?"

Mathias sounded breathless, like he'd been running.

"Hi, Mathias."

"Pascal! I didn't expect to hear from you before I went to work today. I was going to text you before I left so you'd know I was thinking about you."

"Is that why you're out of breath?" Pascal teased.

"Well…," Mathias drawled. "You have to know what thinking about you does to me. Especially right now, when every time I look in a mirror, I see your teeth marks all over my neck."

"I'd apologize, but I don't think you want me to," Pascal replied in kind.

"Nope. You could leave more if you wanted."

If Mathias were there, Pascal would be damn tempted. As it was, they didn't have time before Mathias had to leave for the bar. "Next weekend."

"You aren't really going to make me wait until then, are you?"

He looked at the clock. "If you come up here now, you'll be late for work, and Adrien will be angry with you."

"Talk to me instead," Mathias said. "Tell me what you'd do to me if I was there and we had time."

Pascal swallowed hard. Despite René's comment, this hadn't really been his plan when he called Mathias, but now that Mathias had brought it up, he couldn't think of anything else. "If we had time…."

"All the time in the world." The longing in Mathias's voice hit Pascal hard, stirring an echoing need deep in his gut. He didn't know what kind of vacation time Mathias had at the bank, but they needed to use some of it—rent a cabin somewhere and run away for a long weekend so they could be alone without the constant worry of watching the clock or juggling schedules. A stretch of unrelenting solitude with nothing to do but be together and make love.

"It wouldn't be here. We'd go somewhere romantic. Somewhere away from all the demands of our schedules so we wouldn't have to look at the clock for days," Pascal said. "All we'd have to worry about was eating when we were hungry, sleeping when we were tired, and making love when we were awake."

"It sounds like heaven." Mathias's voice had gone breathless again.

"We're in a cabin," Pascal said, more than happy to elaborate on the theme if it made Mathias sound like that. "There's a fire burning to keep us warm, blankets and cushions from the couch piled into a nest on the floor, and nothing between us but the firelight turning your skin gold."

He closed his eyes and let the image play out in his head. He hadn't taken his time to properly appreciate the picture Mathias made while naked when they'd first had sex. Mathias had been too eager, and Pascal had been afraid to slow down enough for his better judgment to kick in. He'd gotten enough of a glimpse for his imagination to fill in the details now of toned muscles, still slender with youth, exactly what he needed to draw him out of the doldrums of his life. Mathias would reach for him, and he'd go willingly into his arms.

"I'd snuggle in the pillows and pull you down next to me," Mathias said.

Pascal shivered with desire at the image, so close to what he'd had in his own mind. "You wouldn't have to ask me twice. I wouldn't want to be anywhere else but right there with you."

"Not even in me?" Pascal could hear the coquettish smile in Mathias's voice. He groaned low in his throat and headed into the bedroom. He wouldn't survive this conversation fully dressed.

"We'll get there, but remember? We have all the time in the world. If I want to spend hours just nibbling on your neck, I can."

"I won't last hours," Mathias gasped.

"Then I'll just have to get you worked up again," Pascal replied.

"You like knowing you can make me come more than once."

"Guilty as charged," Pascal replied, because hell yeah, he liked it. It was already a huge thrill to know that Mathias wanted him the way he did. To be able to keep that going past his first orgasm… it made Pascal feel like the world's best lover.

"Don't stop."

Pascal wasn't sure if Mathias meant the phone sex or something else, but he found he didn't care. "I won't. I'll nibble all over, little teeth marks on every spot I can reach. And when I'm done with that, I'll start over with my tongue, just to see which you like better."

Mathias's moan carried through the phone, going straight to Pascal's cock. He shed his pants and rubbed his erection through his underwear. He didn't want to rush, but they weren't really at their woodland retreat, and time was passing.

"Your tongue," Mathias said. "Definitely your tongue."

"Anywhere in particular you want it?"

"Anywhere you want to put it," Mathias replied hoarsely.

"That wasn't what I asked. Where do you want it?"

Mathias moaned again. "Rimming me. Flip me over, pull my ass in the air, and eat me out until I can't even hold myself up."

Pascal's stomach lurched at the image. He wanted that. He *needed* that. "The next time we're together. And then, when I've got you sloppy and loose for me, I'll roll over and sit you in my lap. You'll look so good riding me." He slipped his free hand inside his underwear and stroked himself firmly. He hadn't asked what Mathias was doing while they were talking because he could barely handle the conversation and the pictures in his fevered imagination. Adding images of Mathias jerking off or with his fingers in his ass would shatter what little control he had left.

"I'll never keep myself upright," Mathias said around a moan.

"Yes, you will," Pascal replied. "Because you know I want you to. I'll meet you halfway. It'll feel so good. We'll come in a matter of seconds because we'll both be so close. Are you close, Mathias?"

A hiss of breath answered him. "Say my name again."

"Mathias," Pascal repeated. "Sweet, sexy Mathias with the tight ass and big eyes. Smart, sexy Mathias in his business suit and tie." That was a thought to explore next time…. Mathias out of his suit pants with his shirt unbuttoned and his tie loose around his neck. "I dream about you in that suit."

Mathias cursed sharply and cried out. Pascal closed his eyes and imagined what Mathias might look like when he climaxed. He'd made the mistake of taking Mathias from behind the last time so he hadn't been able to see Mathias's face. He wouldn't do that again. He stroked himself a few more times before spilling over his hand. He lay there on his bed, listening to the sound of Mathias's breathing and wished he'd asked Mathias to come up so they could see each other. Even if it had been rushed or left them more frustrated, at least they would have been together.

"We have to figure out this schedule thing," Pascal said. "I want to see you more often."

"I could tell Adrien I can't work on Tuesdays anymore if you can make that your day off consistently," Mathias offered. "It's always a slow night. I wouldn't lose too much income that way, and it would give us one night a week where neither of us had to rush off anywhere."

"I'll talk to Simon. It might be too late for this week, but I'll have him put it on the schedule starting next week," Pascal said.

"It's a date." Pascal could hear Mathias's smile in his tone.

"I can't wait." He'd have to plan something special, whether it was this Tuesday or next, so Mathias would know how much Pascal appreciated the effort. "If René and Benjamin come into the bar tonight, don't let them hassle you too much. René can get a little… overbearing in his teasing at times."

"They were perfect gentlemen last night," Mathias replied.

Pascal doubted that, but at least they hadn't bothered Mathias enough for him to complain about it. "If you say so. Be safe and have a good day at the bank tomorrow."

"I will. Let me know about Tuesday night after you talk to your boss."

"I'll text you as soon as I know." He didn't want to hang up the phone and break the connection between them, but time was passing, and now he needed a shower before he went to the restaurant. "Bye."

"Bye."

The phone beeped to tell him the call had ended, but he stayed where he was, savoring the happiness of the moment.

CHAPTER 18

MATHIAS WOKE up before his alarm on Saturday morning despite having been at Le Salon until way too late Friday night, but he hadn't seen Pascal in a week. They were supposed to meet at nine. Pascal wouldn't tell Mathias what he had planned for the day, only telling him to dress warmly because they would be outside for part of the day. It wasn't miserably cold yet, only nippy, but Mathias had misjudged how the cold could seep into his bones before, and he didn't want to spend the day wishing he had another layer on.

He bounced out of bed with far more energy than usual after such a short night, but he wanted to know what Pascal had planned. He ate and dressed and was ready to go by a little after eight with no idea how to fill the remaining hour. Glancing at his phone, he debated texting Pascal to let him know he was ready early, but he didn't know how long it took Pascal to get ready, and he didn't want to wake him.

Less than ten minutes later, his phone buzzed.

I couldn't sleep. Come up whenever you're ready. I hope I didn't wake you up.

Mathias grinned. *I'll be up in five.*

What a difference a week made! The last time he'd been ready early, he'd looked for excuses to delay so he wouldn't appear overly eager, unsure as he'd been of his reception. Now he pulled on his shoes, grabbed his jacket, and was out the door before a full minute had passed.

He knocked on Pascal's door and waited impatiently for him to open it. "That wasn't five minutes," Pascal said with a smile as he opened the door. Mathias stepped through and straight into a kiss. He'd reply later.

Pascal gathered Mathias into an embrace, returning Mathias's eager kiss with tenderness and teasing. How did he invest so much into such simple contact? Mathias supposed he'd learn someday. For now, he'd enjoy the hell out of it.

"Hi," he said when Pascal finally broke the kiss.

"Hi, yourself."

"I missed you."

Pascal grinned. "They say absence makes the heart grow fonder."

"Maybe, but that was a little too much absence for me."

"I have Tuesdays off from now on, so as long as you don't get dragged into a shift at Le Salon or into something at the bank, we'll see each other then as well as whatever time we can eke out on weekends," Pascal replied. That sounded like heaven to Mathias.

"What are we doing today? I wore good boots for walking, and I grabbed my jacket so I'd be ready for outside time, like you said."

"It's a surprise," Pascal said, the same maddening answer he'd given every time Mathias had asked this week.

Mathias pouted playfully, but Pascal didn't relent, only leaned forward to kiss Mathias again. Mathias leaned into the contact and licked at Pascal's lips in silent invitation.

"Brat." Pascal swatted at Mathias's hip as he stepped back. "If you start that, we'll end up in bed, and you won't get your surprise."

"You did promise me a day spent entirely in bed."

"I did, when we didn't have to worry about getting up that afternoon to go to work," Pascal replied. "We both have to work tonight. That's not conducive to my plans for ruining you for other men."

Mathias shivered. He was pretty sure Pascal had already done that, but he kept the thought to himself. He didn't want Pascal to change his mind about keeping those promises. "You're not making me want to leave your apartment."

"It'll be worth it," Pascal said, guiding Mathias back out the door. "Trust me."

They walked to the underground lot where Pascal kept his car. Pascal opened the door for Mathias and shut it behind him when he climbed in. "I'm dying here," Mathias said when Pascal got in the other side. "Where are we going?"

"Out," Pascal said. "The weather is supposed to be good, sunny and as warm as fourteen degrees. Perfect weather for a drive."

Mathias agreed, but that hadn't answered his question. "But a drive to where?"

"Wherever the road takes us," Pascal said as he pulled out of the garage. "Just relax and enjoy the view. If you see a road that looks interesting, tell me. As long as you tell me soon enough to make the turn."

Pascal took the Autoroute 10 east out of town, pretty much the exact opposite direction Mathias would take to go home if he had the time off and any real desire to visit. He missed his parents and his sisters, but not enough to try to squeeze a six-hour round-trip drive into any time he had to himself. He'd go see them at Christmas. He hadn't had the time to go exploring much around Montréal with the exception of the canoeing trip he and Pascal had taken, but he remembered a little of what he'd learned about the surrounding areas. "The wine country is out this way, right?"

"It is, although I didn't know if you'd be interested in any tastings, so I didn't make plans. We can stop if you want. Most places are open this time of year without reservations, but we don't have to."

"If you didn't make reservations anywhere, then where are we going?"

"I told you. Out of the city. I used to do this with my family when my sister and I were kids. We'd take a day, drive out into the country, look at the leaves changing color, find a little place in some town or another to have lunch, and drive home in time for dinner," Pascal said. "I thought you might like to get out of the city for a few hours. We'll find somewhere that looks interesting for lunch, and it'll either be wonderful, or it'll be a disaster. If it's wonderful, we'll have a great lunch. If it's a disaster, we'll have a good laugh. Either way, we'll go back to town feeling better for having left it for a few hours."

"That's…." Mathias swallowed around the lump of emotion in his throat. "Thank you. That's really thoughtful of you. I love Montréal. It has so much to offer, but sometimes it feels like the concrete is just closing in around me. Mont Royal is nice, but it's still in the city."

"You're welcome."

Mathias reached across the space between them to take Pascal's hand. Pascal squeezed back and twined their fingers together. They drove in comfortable silence as the city fell away and the countryside opened up around them. It was less wooded than the area around home, but the trees along the road had taken on the colors of fall—rich red, brilliant orange, vibrant yellow, a riot of color that reminded him of home. He hadn't realized just how tense he'd become until it started bleeding away. "Do you mind?" he asked, reaching for the button to roll down the window. It was cool outside, but he needed the fresh air.

"Go ahead. I wore layers."

Mathias lowered the window a little less than halfway and inhaled deeply. They weren't far enough away from the city for it to smell strongly of the countryside yet, but just the lack of overwhelming exhaust fumes was already a huge improvement. He closed his eyes and reveled in the wind on his face. Pascal turned off the autoroute and onto a country lane leading toward Farnham. As they continued, the air changed, becoming more humid, with the scent of fallen leaves. Mathias took another deep breath and exhaled slowly. "I don't think I realized how much I needed this. I don't have a car, mostly because I don't need one." He couldn't have afforded one anyway. "I'm outside all the time, either going for a run or on my way to or from work, but it's not the same."

"No, it's not the same. I've always lived in Montréal, but when we were younger, my parents would rent a place for us in the summer. We'd take a month and go away. I spent my days running in the woods north of the city. I miss that sometimes."

"Is that why you travel the way you do?"

Pascal glanced over at him and smiled before turning his attention back to the road. "Sometimes. The Inca Trail was certainly a back-to-nature trip, but they aren't all. There's nothing out of the city about going to Prague."

"True, although it's out of *your* city."

"It depends on what you need out of a vacation, then," Pascal said. "Is a change of urban scenery enough, or do you really need out of the city altogether?"

"Right now, out of the city altogether, but it'll be years before I have the time or money to take the kind of vacations you do. I'll have a week off here and there, but that's not the way you travel."

"It's not the way I *traveled*." Pascal stressed the past tense so earnestly that Mathias couldn't help but smile. "I traveled that way because I had no reason not to. I'd be fine with weekend getaways at a lodge somewhere. A little cross-country skiing or snowshoeing, then a warm fire and a glass of wine. That would be a wonderful winter getaway."

It sounded lovely, if out of Mathias's price range. He didn't mention that, though. Pascal wasn't actually suggesting they should go away together for the weekend anytime soon. Maybe by the time he brought it up for real, Mathias would have managed to save enough money to make it affordable.

"You can close your eyes and rest a bit more if you want," Pascal said when Mathias didn't reply to his comment. "It'll be a bit longer before we get to Farnham. We can stop there and wander around a bit, or we can drive deeper into the wine country before we stop. It's up to you."

"I don't know the area at all," Mathias replied, "so you have to tell me what's interesting. I'm just happy to be with you and out of the city."

"Then let's stop at Farnham. I thought we could have lunch in Dunham and then see whether we're up to stopping at a winery before we head back. But that gives us the morning to fill."

"That sounds perfect."

PASCAL FOUND a place to park in Farnham near the church. They zipped up their jackets and wandered along the river. The streets lined with elms were quiet, a few locals going about their morning shopping. Mathias slipped his hand into Pascal's as they strolled along the lanes. He took a deep breath and exhaled slowly.

"You okay?" Pascal asked. "You've been doing a lot of that."

"A lot of what?"

"Deep breaths and almost sighs."

Mathias laughed. "Sorry. Didn't mean to worry you. I'm enjoying the smell of the country. It's very relaxing, reminds me of home."

"You need to go home," Pascal said. "Take a weekend off from the bar and go see your family. It would do you good."

It probably would, but that wasn't an option right now. "I'll see them at Christmas. I don't have a car, so they'd have to come get me, which makes a long weekend really not feasible." He kept his voice light. He wouldn't always have to scramble to make ends meet. When his training was over, he'd get a substantial raise, enough to quit at Le Salon completely and still be able to afford a car. He just had to make it another eighteen months.

"What about Thanksgiving?"

Mathias shrugged. "I'll enjoy the day off. Sleep late, that sort of thing."

"You could come with me to my sister's house," Pascal offered.

"Really?" Mathias said before thinking the better of it. "I wouldn't want to impose."

"It wouldn't be an imposition. I invited you. I got a lecture last weekend from my parents for not bringing you with me to lunch."

"You told them about me?" Mathias flinched at how unsure he sounded, but the words had already slipped out.

"My parents know I'm gay," Pascal said. "They considered Robert their son too, before he died. They're happy I've finally found someone again."

Mathias leaned closer to Pascal, trying to take that in, to figure out how it fit into his image of their relationship. His parents knew he was gay too, but he hadn't told them he was seeing anyone seriously. Until a week ago, he hadn't been sure it was as serious as he wanted it to be, and even now he hadn't thought they were at the "meet the parents" stage. "That's... we were... I didn't think...." He stopped the babble of words with a deep breath and started over. "I'd be happy to spend Thanksgiving with your family if you're comfortable with that. I know I'm probably not what they had in mind for you, but I won't let you down."

Pascal stopped walking and turned to face Mathias, his face as serious as during their talk last weekend. "The only one who gets to decide what's right for me is me. They know that and will be happy to meet you because I'm happy with you. I told them you work at the BMO and that we live in the same building. They're going to look at you and see an up-and-coming professional, and they're going to wonder what you see in me, not the other way around."

There it was again, that hint of self-recrimination, as if Pascal's choice to be a waiter somehow made him less in his own eyes. "We had that discussion already, but I'll say it again if I need to." He paused to see if Pascal would stop him, but the silence was all too telling. "You see yourself as 'just a waiter,' but I see someone who has picked a career and made something of it. I think I told you my boss won't have business dinners anywhere but your restaurant. We have one coming up in a few weeks. I'm actually invited this time."

"Tell me when you're coming in. I'll make sure your group is well taken care of. I may not be able to seat you in my section, but I can make sure you're with someone who will give you great service."

"From everything I've heard and everything you've said, I'm sure everyone you work with gives good service. Although I wouldn't complain if you were the one to take care of us. I'd love to see you at work."

The lines around Pascal's mouth deepened as he frowned. Mathias cursed inwardly. Wrong choice of thing to say. "I'd spend the entire dinner trying not to jump you."

Pascal laughed at that, easing the tension in Mathias's gut. "There's nothing particularly attractive about a white apron over black slacks. Trust me, you aren't missing anything."

"I'll be the judge of that," Mathias replied. "After all, it's my buttons you'll be pushing."

Pascal squeezed his hand. "If you say so."

If they'd been in Montréal, Mathias wouldn't have hesitated to pull Pascal into a kiss, but out in the country as they were, attitudes changed more slowly. It might be fine, or it might not. He'd save the kiss until they got back to the car.

CHAPTER 19

"WHAT'S WITH the look on your face?" Louis asked when Mathias walked into the bank on Monday morning.

"He invited me to spend Thanksgiving with his family," Mathias blurted out.

"That's good, though, right?" Louis asked. "It means he's serious about your relationship."

It was a good thing, but that didn't make Mathias more prepared to deal with it. "What am I supposed to wear? What if they ask where we met? I mean, we live in the same building, but we actually met at the bar, and what if they don't like me or think I'm too young for him or not good enough for him or—"

"Breathe, Mathias. You're working yourself up for nothing."

Mathias obediently took a deep breath. "I'm being ridiculous."

"It's not ridiculous to be nervous about meeting his parents. Just don't make it out to be worse than it really is. If he invited you, he obviously thinks it will be fine."

The reminder relaxed Mathias somewhat. Pascal hadn't asked until Mathias mentioned not going home, but he *had* asked. He could have simply stayed silent and accepted it when Mathias said he'd stay in and enjoy the day off from the bar, but he hadn't. He'd invited Mathias to spend Thanksgiving with him, and he'd told his parents about them already.

"That still doesn't answer the question of what to wear," Mathias joked to lighten the mood. He hadn't meant to tell Louis quite as much as he had. He certainly didn't want to say more.

Louis laughed. "You'll have to ask him that question. Every family is different. My family is all about being comfortable—jeans and T-shirts or hoodies, depending on the temperature—but I dated someone whose family all wore suits or dresses on Thanksgiving. He won't think it odd if you ask. Just tell him you want to make a good first impression."

That part would be relatively easy. Pascal would understand his wanting to make a good impression. He hadn't seemed worried about his parents' reaction, but he wouldn't want Mathias to make a bad impression. The rest was harder to control, though. He couldn't make himself older than he was. He couldn't make himself less of a newcomer to Montréal, less of a country kid out of his depth in the city. He couldn't make his family less working class or his speech less accented. Pascal spoke with a smooth Montréal accent in French and no hint of a French accent in English, nothing like the thicker accent of the countryside where Mathias had grown up. No one at the bank commented on it, but he saw the occasional look, especially from the ones obviously from the city. They expected a more polished accent from someone in a professional position. If Pascal's parents had the same reaction, would it ruin things with Pascal? Pascal had never seemed bothered by it, but that didn't mean his parents shared his open-mindedness.

"I know that look. You're worrying over things you can't change. It won't help, and if you're nervous, it'll make it harder to enjoy. Don't do that to Pascal."

"He's just so perfect, and I'm… not."

"You realize neither of those statements is accurate, right? I'm sure he's wonderful, but he isn't perfect. No one is. And you're not nearly as bad as you think you are, or he wouldn't be interested in you in the first place. Unless you're still stuck on the idea that he just wants you for sex."

It would be easy to believe except Pascal didn't act that way. They'd come back from the drive in the country too late to do anything but kiss good-bye before they had to get ready for work, and they hadn't managed to see each other on Sunday. They had a date for tomorrow night, but knowing Pascal, they'd go out somewhere instead of going to bed. He'd have to make sure they made it back in time to have a little fun before the night ended, or he'd start wondering if Pascal still wanted him instead of fearing he only wanted sex. "He wouldn't take the time to plan such nice dates if he only wanted sex."

"What did you do this weekend? Something fun?"

Mathias jumped at the change of subject and settled in to tell Louis about their drive on Saturday. He'd worry about the rest later.

A WEEK later he wasn't any closer to being comfortable with going with Pascal for Thanksgiving despite Pascal's repeated assurances that his parents would love Mathias. He'd settled on nice slacks and a button-down shirt but no tie or sports coat for dinner. Pascal said it wasn't anything super formal, but Mathias didn't want to show up in jeans. Even if Pascal dressed that way, he was part of the family, not a newcomer on trial. Their date on Tuesday had gone as well as Mathias could have hoped. He hadn't even had to convince Pascal to take him to bed at the end of the night. It wasn't the rush to the finish line of their first night together, but it had ended with his knees around his ears in a gratifyingly short period of time. He smiled at the memory, hoping tonight would end the same way. Pascal was a masterful lover, and Mathias wanted more, the sooner the better. It would be his reward for surviving the next few hours.

A knock on the door interrupted his nervous brooding. He grabbed his coat and headed toward the door.

"Hi." Pascal stood outside his door in a royal-blue shirt open at the neck and black slacks, his coat over his arm. Mathias breathed a sigh of relief. He'd picked the right outfit "You look very nice."

"So do you," Pascal replied, giving Mathias a thorough once-over. "Ready to go?"

"You're sure this is a good idea?"

"You don't have to come if you don't want to." The hurt tone of Pascal's voice decided Mathias.

"No, it's not that. Of course I want to meet your family. I'm just nervous. I want them to like me."

"I'm pretty sure that the fact that I'm smiling will be enough to win them over." Pascal slipped his arm through Mathias's as they walked down to the garage where Pascal kept his car. "According to my sister, I haven't done enough of that the past few years."

Mathias liked knowing he could make Pascal smile. He waited while Pascal unlocked the car, but as soon as they were both settled, he leaned across the gearshift to kiss Pascal tenderly.

The warm feeling lasted through the drive to Pascal's sister's house. When Pascal parked in front of a little house in the Côte-des-Neiges neighborhood, all his nerves returned. Côte-des-Neiges might not have been the most expensive neighborhood in the city, but it was expensive enough. He'd come a long way from La Tuque, that was for sure.

Before they could even get out of the car, the front door flew open, and a little tow-headed girl came running out. "Uncle Pascal!"

The smile on Pascal's face stole Mathias's breath. He would have said he'd seen Pascal smile before, but it had never been this bright or carefree. If getting Pascal's parents to like him meant making Pascal smile like that, he had a lot still to learn.

"Hello, Chantal. How's my little songbird?" Pascal caught his niece in a big hug and swung her around in a circle a couple of times, to the chorus of her delighted giggles. The musical sound fit her name perfectly.

"I learned a new song at music lessons. I'll sing it for you after dinner. Maman says I have to wait until after we've eaten before I show off."

Pascal laughed. "Chantal, this is my friend, Mathias. I bet he'd love to hear you sing later."

"Hi, Chantal." Mathias offered his hand. Chantal shook it with a very serious expression on her face.

"Hello, sir," Chantal replied politely.

Mathias wanted to tell her he wasn't old enough to be "sir," but that wasn't his call to make without talking to Pascal's sister first.

"Let's go inside. We can get acquainted where it's warmer."

Chantal slipped her hand into Pascal's and led him toward the door, chattering a mile a minute about her friends at school and their new class pet. Mathias trailed along behind, feeling more left out by the minute. He didn't begrudge Pascal the attention he paid to Chantal, not really. He just needed a bit of Pascal's attention for himself to settle his jangling nerves.

They were taking off their coats when Pascal's sister came into the entrance hall. She kissed Pascal's cheek, sent her daughter off on an errand, and offered her hand to Mathias. "You must be Mathias. Welcome to chaos. I'm Sylvie."

"Nice to meet you, Sylvie," Mathias said. "Thank you for including me in Thanksgiving."

"You're welcome, although you may not say that by the time the day is over." She turned to Pascal. "Maman is not having a good day."

Pascal sighed and turned to Mathias. "My mother has a kind of dementia. Some days she's fine and the same woman who raised us, some days she thinks we're still kids but is otherwise mostly coherent, and some days she doesn't know any of us or where she is at all."

"Today is one of the days when she thinks it's twenty years ago," Sylvie said. "She's called me by her sister's name twice, and she's convinced Chantal is me. She keeps asking where you are. I told her you'd be here soon, and she wanted to know whose house you'd gone to on Thanksgiving."

"I'm sorry," Pascal said to Mathias. "It's been a long time since she had a bad spell. I was hoping that would continue a little longer."

"It'll be fine," Mathias said.

"She may not remember that I told her about you. She may not remember I'm gay. The last time she had a bad spell, she kept on about how I needed to meet a nice girl and settle down. She wasn't nasty when I told her I wasn't interested in women—it was more like she didn't hear me—but it's not the way I want you to meet her either."

It wasn't the way Mathias wanted to meet her, but he didn't have much choice in the matter unless he backed out now, which was pretty much impossible since Pascal had driven. He could probably catch the bus, but he didn't know the routes or how often they'd be running since it was Thanksgiving. He'd just have to suck it up and deal with it.

"They're in the kitchen," Sylvie said. "I can get Papa first, if you think that will be easier."

"No, because then Maman will fuss about that. If she's slipped back in time, not out of it completely, that won't have changed."

"She runs the family?" Mathias asked with a grin.

"Like you wouldn't believe."

Mathias chuckled, but he could imagine how much harder on everyone that made her dementia. Pascal slipped his hand into Mathias's and headed deeper into the house. The house wasn't a showplace. It was clearly lived in and loved. Chantal's toys were scattered around the living room, but the clutter of everyday life couldn't disguise the underlying elegance of the building. Sylvie didn't seem hung up on it, but this was the life Mathias aspired to, not the one he was currently living.

Pascal was comfortable here, given the way he didn't wait for Sylvie, and he didn't think any less of Mathias for his second job—or even for the fact that he needed a second job to live on rue Sainte-Catherine.

They walked into a modern kitchen, a bit at odds with the rest of the house but equipped with everything a cook could need. An older couple sat at the table. The man looked so much like Pascal that Mathias would have known who they were even without the context. He smiled and waited for Pascal to introduce them.

"Maman, Papa, this is Mathias. I told you about him the other day," Pascal said. "Mathias, my parents, Julien and Marguerite."

Marguerite's gaze flicked from Pascal's face to their joined hands. "Pascal! Why are you holding his hand? Where is Robert? You made promises. Your father and I raised you better than that."

"Maman," Sylvie interrupted before she could say more or Pascal could reply, "you're confused again. Come in the other room with me." She pulled her mother to her feet and ushered her toward the door.

"Stop that, Sylvie. Pascal is behaving reprehensibly. You can't possibly condone this. Did you know he was bringing someone else to Thanksgiving?"

Sylvie got her mother out of the room and the door closed before she replied, but Mathias didn't see any way that conversation could finish well.

"I apologize," Pascal's father said, rising slowly. "Marguerite doesn't always remember things. Usually she remembers the important ones, though. Please don't take her words to heart. If she were herself, she would never have said them. She was quite put out with Pascal for not bringing you to lunch the day he first mentioned you."

"That's kind of you to say." No words, however kind, could soothe the sudden ache in Mathias's chest, though. He was the replacement. No matter how long he was around, he would always be the one Pascal picked when he couldn't have the one he wanted.

Julien snorted. "I'm not in the habit of being 'kind.' Just ask Pascal. I prefer to tell the truth. Then no one has any question about where they stand."

Mathias glanced at Pascal, who looked stricken but nodded at his father's words.

"Then it's a pleasure to meet you." Mathias summoned a smile and put his best effort into meaning it.

CHAPTER 20

PASCAL LISTENED to his father and Mathias talk, but the conversation was a buzz in his ears. He couldn't believe his mother had said those things. He needed to pull Mathias aside and apologize at the very least. He could offer to leave. Chantal wouldn't understand, but Sylvie and Bertrand wouldn't blame him for taking Mathias and leaving.

Sylvie came back in before he could get his head back in the game. She took the scene in with a single glance and grabbed Pascal's arm. "Maman is lying down. I convinced her that some rest would make things better. I don't know if it'll help her memories, but it will give us a break. Is he all right?"

"Would you be?"

"I'd have already run for the hills," Sylvie said. "So either he's made of sterner stuff, or he's too shocked to react yet. Maman is in our room. You can go in the spare room if you want to talk to him in private."

"Thanks, Sylvie."

"Her reaction wasn't a reflection of reality. You know that. If you'd done what she thinks you did, it would be justified, but you didn't, and when she remembers that, she'll be fine with Mathias."

But would Mathias be fine with her? The dementia wouldn't ever get any better. Oh, she'd have good days and bad days, but it would get worse, and the bad days would outnumber the good days, and they'd run the risk of a similar confrontation every time Mathias came to a family function. Mathias would be completely within his right to refuse to ever come with Pascal to see his family again. Pascal wouldn't even blame him. No one in their right mind would want to deal with that kind of confrontation a second time.

Bertrand came in with Chantal, providing a distraction for Papa, which let Pascal pull Mathias aside. "Come with me."

Mathias followed mechanically.

"I am *so* sorry," he said when they were alone in the hallway. "If I'd known she would react that way, I never would have suggested we spend Thanksgiving here."

"You couldn't have known," Mathias said, but his voice sounded hollow to Pascal's ears.

"Whatever you're thinking, you're wrong," Pascal said, though he wouldn't blame Mathias for running away screaming. "Do you want to leave? We can find somewhere else to have dinner. I'm sure there's a restaurant with a table available."

"No, that's not fair to you," Mathias replied. "You should be able to spend Thanksgiving with your family. I can go. I'm sure there's a bus that will take me home."

Pascal shook his head vehemently. Mathias couldn't leave like this. Pascal had brought him here. If Mathias wanted to leave, Pascal would be a gentleman and take him home. "I will take you home if that's what you want. I wouldn't want to stay if I were you after the way Maman acted."

"No, it's fine. I'm prepared for it now. It just caught me off guard."

Pascal hugged Mathias tightly. He couldn't possibly deserve Mathias's acceptance of the situation, but he wouldn't look a gift horse in the mouth. If Mathias was willing to stay and put up with the uncertainty that was Maman's behavior, Pascal would be grateful and make sure he knew it.

"Now that we know how she's acting today, we'll try to run interference for you," Pascal said. "Stay close to Bertrand or Sylvie if you can't stay with me. I'll do my best to keep her attention on me."

"You don't have to do that," Mathias said. "I'm an adult. I can handle a little disapproval."

"But you shouldn't have to," Pascal protested. "There's nothing to disapprove of. None of her upset is justified."

"You did make promises to Robert."

"Yes, I did, and if he were still alive, I'd still be doing my best to keep them, but he isn't, and we talked about it before he died. He said I was too young to lock myself in a mausoleum with him. He said the best tribute I could give his memory was to live a long, full, happy life. If anything, I'm finally keeping my promise to him by being here with you."

That was dangerously close to a declaration that Mathias probably had no interest in hearing after the hour they'd had, so Pascal stopped the flow of words before he could say things he couldn't unsay.

MATHIAS COULDN'T say later how he'd made it through the rest of the afternoon, but Sylvie, Bertrand, and Julien did everything they could to keep Marguerite from making another scene, and Pascal didn't leave his side for more than a minute until it was time to leave. He followed Pascal out to the car, still feeling hollowed out inside. He hated being the source of tension. Everyone had tried to help, but how long would it be before they started resenting the work it took to have him there?

"Hey," Pascal said when they were both seated. "Are you okay?"

Mathias summoned a smile, hoping it looked less forced than it felt. "Just tired. I was out late at the bar last night, and I didn't want to be late for Thanksgiving, so I didn't sleep in today."

"You would have been happier staying home and sleeping in. I really am sorry."

"It's not your fault," Mathias said. "I know that."

"If it makes any difference, I was glad to have you there. It was the first Thanksgiving in a long time where I didn't feel a little left out."

"Left out?" Mathias couldn't imagine Pascal feeling that way surrounded by his family. They had laughed and joked with him all day, including him in every conversation and even making an effort to explain things to Mathias.

Pascal shrugged. "Sylvie and Bertrand, Maman and Papa, Robert and me. It was always supposed to be three couples, not two couples and me. They never meant to do it, but it still felt like I was odd man out. Even with Maman having a difficult day, I didn't feel that way today."

Mathias couldn't imagine his presence having helped anything, but he'd take what he could get.

"It's not late yet. Do you have time to come upstairs with me, or do you need to get to sleep early?"

Mathias considered the question for a moment. Pascal might not have couched it in those terms, but going upstairs with him would end in sex. A nice, sweaty round of sex to leave him mindless and boneless might be just what he needed to relax. A consolation prize, even if he hadn't managed to make a good first impression on Pascal's family. "I have time. Like you said, it's not late."

Pascal reached across the gearshift and squeezed Mathias's hand. "Thank you. I want to make up for my mother's bad behavior if I can."

Mathias squeezed back, the contact soothing some of the sting he still felt from Madame Larocque's reaction to him. He could tell himself all day long that the rest of Pascal's family didn't feel the same way. It still hurt.

They passed the rest of the drive in silence. Pascal parked in the garage and reached for Mathias's hand again as soon as they had both gotten out of the car.

They climbed the steps side by side. Pascal never loosened his grip on Mathias's hand, but neither did he push Mathias against the wall to kiss him as he had done other times they climbed those stairs together. Mathias wasn't sure what to make of that, but as long as Pascal didn't let go, he wouldn't either.

When they got to Pascal's apartment and he started fumbling one-handed with the key, Mathias laughed. "You can let go long enough to open the door. I promise I won't disappear in the time it takes you to get us inside. I'm as invested in being here as you are."

Pascal smiled at the quip, but it didn't reach his eyes, much to Mathias's dismay. Had he said something wrong? Was the invitation upstairs for something other than sex? Pascal had said he wanted to make up for his mother's behavior, which implied something good, but that didn't actually have to mean sex, now that Mathias thought about it. His hand felt cold when Pascal released it to open the door and usher him inside.

"Hey," Pascal said after closing the door. "What are you thinking? You look worried."

"Nothing," Mathias said. He summoned a smile and stepped close enough to Pascal to rub against him invitingly. "You've got me upstairs. What are you going to do with me?"

Pascal wrapped his arms around Mathias and leaned in to kiss him, the contact so tender Mathias started worrying again. They had kissed dozens of times, but it had always been different. Hot and a little hard and definitely hungry, on both sides. This wasn't any of those things.

He tried to relax into the kiss, because while it wasn't what he'd expected, Pascal didn't pull away either. He kept Mathias tight against him and kept kissing him, gentle presses of mouth to mouth, little sips of pleasure so different from the usual wave of lust. Mathias parted his lips in invitation, but Pascal didn't respond. Instead he moved away from Mathias's mouth to coast over his cheeks, his eyes, the bridge of his nose.

"Pascal?"

Pascal hummed in his throat but didn't stop what he was doing. As long as he wasn't stopping, Mathias could be patient. The heat between them wouldn't stay banked forever. Pascal had proven that every time they'd ended up in bed. He walked his fingers up Pascal's arm, heading for his chest with every intention of encouraging a faster pace, but Pascal caught his hand and returned it to the back of his neck. Mathias pouted at being forestalled, but Pascal just kissed him again with the same tender, undemanding pressure.

Pascal nipped at Mathias's lower lip and pulled back. "Let me take your coat. If you're planning on staying a while, of course."

Mathias wasn't planning on going anywhere except Pascal's bed for the next several hours. He pulled his coat off and started to toss it on the table near the door, but Pascal took it from him and hung it in the closet behind the door. "No need to rush, is there?"

"I suppose not."

"Good. Then let me do this right."

Mathias didn't know how it could be any more "right" than it had already been, but he'd long since accepted that Pascal had more experience than he did. Pascal hadn't given him a reason to complain so far. He could trust him tonight too.

Pascal reached for him again. Mathias stepped right back into the embrace since that was exactly where he wanted to be. He tipped his head up for another kiss. Pascal gave him a quick peck but didn't linger. Instead he guided Mathias down the hall to the bedroom.

That was progress.

Mathias grabbed the hem of his shirt as soon as they crossed the threshold, but Pascal stopped him. "Not rushing, remember?"

"We can 'not rush' naked, can't we?" Mathias asked.

Pascal snickered. "Sure, that will happen. I'm not made of stone. Once I get you naked, I'm going to forget all my good intentions, and it'll be over before we really get started. Just like all the other times we've ended up in bed."

"You haven't heard me complaining yet."

Pascal traced Mathias's jaw with one long finger. "No, I haven't, but that doesn't mean you don't deserve better. You aren't some piece of ass I picked up in a bar, and I refuse to treat you that way again."

"You haven't ever treated me that way," Mathias protested.

"Then you've never been treated right."

"Or you don't treat anyone as badly as you think you do," Mathias replied.

Pascal shrugged. "Not worth arguing over. Come here and let me do this right."

Mathias walked to Pascal, hands at his side, and waited. He really didn't know what Pascal thought he'd done wrong. If anything, Mathias had been gratified by the way Pascal hadn't been able to resist him for long. It had made him feel attractive and powerful in a way few other things did, but this was clearly important to Pascal. He'd already decided he could be patient. If Pascal thought he could do better than the other times they'd had sex, it would be well worth Mathias's while.

Pascal twined the fingers of one hand with Mathias's and braced their clasped hands at the small of Mathias's back. He lifted Mathias's other hand to his lips and kissed the palm lightly before nipping at the thick muscle at the base of his thumb. Mathias shivered. How had he reached the age of twenty-four and not known that was an erogenous zone?

Pascal smiled against his skin—Mathias could feel it in the way his lips moved. He might have protested being a source of amusement, but Pascal lifted his hand higher and sucked on the inside of Mathias's wrist, sending another shiver through him. Fuck, he didn't know his body at all.

"You take a piece of ass to bed, you prep him, and you fuck him," Pascal said against his skin, each movement of his lips, each burst of breath a new titillation. "Maybe you suck him a bit or he sucks you, in the name of foreplay, but it's all about getting off. Sure, you both enjoy it. That's kind of the point. But it could be any body in the bed with you. You aren't any body to me, which means finding all the places that are special. What makes *you* feel good?"

Mathias couldn't harness the brainpower to reply. Then again, he wasn't sure what he'd say even if he could make his brain cooperate. If

Pascal had asked an hour ago, he'd have said having someone suck him off or play with his ass. He certainly wouldn't have said having Pascal suck on his wrist or bite at the base of his thumb, as Pascal had already shown him. Now he wondered what other secrets his body had.

"You don't have to tell me," Pascal said when Mathias didn't answer. "I'll enjoy finding out for myself."

He guided Mathias to the bed and urged him down onto the mattress. Mathias clung to Pascal's hand when he straightened. "Don't worry. I'm not going anywhere," Pascal said. "I'm just going to turn the lamp on and the overhead light off."

Mathias tracked Pascal's movements around the room. He moved with the same easy grace as ever, nothing in his body language suggesting he had any idea how he had turned Mathias's world upside down in the past minute. Feeling suddenly young and insecure, Mathias scrambled to sit against the headboard. He'd be on Pascal's level that way instead of beneath him. Not that he wouldn't end up beneath him before the night was over, but by then they'd be back on familiar territory.

"You moved," Pascal said with a soft smile when he returned to the bed.

"I thought it would be easier this way." The words sounded weak to Mathias's ear, but Pascal didn't challenge them. He simply reached for Mathias's hand again and sucked on one of his fingers. Mathias moaned at the suction, easily imagining Pascal's lips around a different appendage. Except now that Pascal had planted the idea in his head, Mathias wanted to know what he'd been missing. He flexed his finger against Pascal's tongue, trying to tease him back a little. Pascal looked up and winked at him before sliding Mathias's finger into his mouth to the second knuckle. Mathias shifted on the bed as his cock started to fill. He didn't reach down to adjust himself, but if Pascal kept this up, he'd have to before long.

Pascal switched to Mathias's middle finger, using his tongue more this time rather than sucking. Mathias gasped and closed his eyes, but that only intensified the sensations. He carded his fingers through Pascal's short hair, mussing the usually perfect style. He wouldn't know where to begin returning Pascal's attentions, short of copying him directly, but he had to touch. He needed that much grounding.

Pascal switched fingers again to suck on Mathias's ring finger. As he did, he worked open the button on the sleeve of Mathias's shirt and rolled back the cuff. Mathias fought down the urge to blush. They'd been naked together. Pascal had been balls-deep in his ass more than once. Those few inches of bare skin shouldn't even register, and yet he felt somehow more exposed now than he had when they were fucking.

Pascal pulled off Mathias's finger and studied him intently. "Fingers, palm, wrist… you have sensitive hands. I wonder if your feet are as sensitive."

"My feet have been sweating in socks all day. You don't want to suck on them."

"Maybe not tonight," Pascal conceded, "but I can try other things."

"Do you have a foot fetish?"

"Not particularly, but the real question is whether you do."

Mathias started to say of course he didn't, but Pascal's piercing gaze stopped the reply before it formed. "I don't know. Apparently I have sensitive hands, but I didn't know it before tonight."

Pascal grinned, sending a fresh curl of need through Mathias's gut. "Let's see what else we can discover."

Pascal slipped off one of Mathias's shoes and slid his pants leg up to roll down his sock, leaving Mathias's nerves jumping each place Pascal's knuckles came into contact with his skin. It was just skin, for Christ's sake. Just his calf and shin and ankle. It wasn't like Pascal was touching him in any particularly intimate way. And yet….

Pascal set the sock and shoe aside and took Mathias's foot in both hands. Mathias's gut clenched in anticipation. He was sure people had touched his feet before now—doctors, shoe salesmen—but never with so much import. Pascal stroked across the top of Mathias's foot, making every nerve ending jump. He nearly pulled away because it tickled, but Pascal's grip on his ankle tightened, and he stroked again, more firmly this time. That felt better. Still way more intimate than Mathias could explain, but not ticklish.

"That way?" Pascal asked.

Mathias nodded.

Pascal repeated the firmer caress, then wrapped his hand around Mathias's foot to massage the sole. Mathias moaned.

"I'll add your feet to the list, or is that just because you spend so much time on them at the bar? I can give you a massage later if that was a relaxation moan rather than an arousal moan."

Mathias shook his head. He didn't know which it was, really, but it didn't matter. Pascal had his hands on him, and it felt good. He'd worry later about whether he had a heretofore unknown foot fetish or he just needed a good massage.

Pascal winked at him as he pressed his thumb into Mathias's arch. With his other hand, he traced the skin beneath the hem of Mathias's pants. Every hair on Mathias's leg stood straight up. He leaned back against the pillows and shifted to make space for his growing erection. Pascal arched an eyebrow and stared pointedly at the bulge beneath Mathias's fly. "See? I told you I could find ways to make you feel good without going straight to fucking."

"I see," Mathias replied breathlessly. "What else can you show me?" Before meeting Pascal, he would have said those words with cocky challenge, sure he didn't have anything else to learn. Now he meant them with every fiber of his being. He was so far out of his league, but he was going to take full advantage of Pascal's willingness to teach him.

"Let's find out."

Mathias shivered in anticipation.

Pascal gave the top of his foot one last teasing stroke before moving over Mathias on hands and knees. For a moment, Mathias thought it was all over, that Pascal would strip him and take advantage of the position, but he didn't touch Mathias at all. The lack of contact only heightened Mathias's awareness of how effectively caged he was between Pascal's hands and knees. His lips parted on a silent gasp as he waited to see what Pascal would do.

Pascal leaned forward to touch his lips to Mathias's jaw and then downward toward the collar of his shirt. Mathias tipped his head to the side to make it easier for Pascal to reach his goal, whatever that might be. He expected Pascal to suck or bite at his pulse point or his Adam's apple, the spots Mathias would have gone for if their positions had been reversed. He should have known Pascal had something else in mind.

The touch of a single finger at the hollow of his throat electrified Mathias. He hadn't worn a tie, so his shirt had two buttons open, and Pascal traced the line of fabric, the contact so whisper light Mathias could barely feel it. It aroused him more than any firmer touch would have done as he arched into the elusive caress. Pascal moved with him, never letting him achieve what he thought he wanted.

"Shh," Pascal whispered against his ear. "You know I'll give you what you need."

"But when?" Mathias asked back just as softly.

"When waiting a second longer would break you." Pascal sucked Mathias's earlobe into his mouth.

Mathias let out a shaky sigh. "That's not going to be hard."

Pascal pulled back and studied Mathias's face intently before giving him a wicked grin. Fast as lightning, he reached between Mathias's spread thighs and cupped his cock in a firm grip. Mathias bucked up with a hoarse shout. "It feels pretty hard to me," Pascal teased.

"Fuck," Mathias gasped.

"Later," Pascal replied, releasing his grip and returning his hand to its place by Mathias's shoulder. The sensation of being surrounded increased tenfold for having been momentarily absent. Mathias panted as he tried to relax and remember how to be patient.

"Bastard."

"No, you met my parents today."

The reminder cooled Mathias's ardor somewhat, but before he could think of a reply, Pascal kissed him, deep and hard this time, everything Mathias had been expecting earlier and hadn't received. To have it now, after countless minutes of barely there caresses, made his head spin. He moaned into the kiss, trying to meet Pascal halfway, but he couldn't do anything other than lie there beneath the sensual onslaught of Pascal's lips and tongue. He couldn't even get his arms around Pascal at the angle he was leaning over Mathias. All he could do was take it—and love every second of it.

When Pascal broke the kiss, Mathias tried to follow him, but Pascal stopped him with that single finger against his chest. Mathias froze, waiting to see what came next. Pascal held his gaze as he flipped open the third and fourth buttons on Mathias's shirt, not enough to open it completely, but enough to reveal more of his skin to the cool air in the apartment. Mathias shivered, hoping Pascal would keep going or would slip a hand beneath the fabric to find his nipples, anything to ramp up the sensual need he was feeling. Pascal had other plans—not that Mathias was surprised at this point—tracing up and down

Mathias's breastbone. He paused at each bump like it was as sensitive as Mathias's nipples. It felt good because it was Pascal's hands on him, but it didn't carry the same surprising jolt he'd gotten from his hands and feet.

"No?" Pascal asked after a moment.

"Not as much."

"Then we'll try other things. No two people are exactly alike when it comes to their erogenous zones."

"Some things are pretty universal," Mathias said.

"Yes, but the idea is to find the things that make you special, remember? Anyone can grab your ass. I want to find the things no one else knows about you."

"You're finding things I didn't even know," Mathias admitted.

"Even better."

The pride and possessiveness in Pascal's voice made Mathias squirm. He hadn't done anything to earn this kind of attention and devotion. He only hoped Pascal didn't change his mind later, because Mathias was already addicted.

Pascal finished unbuttoning his shirt, but he didn't move his arms enough for Mathias to shrug it off. Instead he folded it open with care, framing Mathias's chest, and rocked back on his heels to look at Mathias speculatively.

"You've seen me naked before," Mathias said, feeling far more naked now than he had with no clothes on and Pascal fucking him.

"I have. This time I'm paying attention."

Mathias remembered Pascal's intent stare as he'd followed Mathias into the bedroom, ass framed by his jockstrap. If that hadn't been paying attention, Mathias didn't know what was, but he didn't have the wherewithal to argue right now. He tensed as Pascal followed the curve of his side with the same delicacy that he'd used to start on all of Mathias's body. "Tickles," he said through clenched teeth.

Pascal grinned. "We'll try that another time. Tonight I want you writhing on my bed for other reasons."

Mathias bucked his hips in blatant invitation. "Give me a reason, then."

Pascal smirked and grabbed Mathias's hand. Mathias let out a startled moan before Pascal ever got his lips around Mathias's fingers, just from the remembered sensation. "You're still thinking so literally. We really have to work on that."

"I'm not thinking," Mathias grumbled.

Pascal laughed. "Good. Lie back and let me make you feel."

If he felt any more, he'd explode from it, but he didn't tell Pascal that. Pascal might stop if he did, and that didn't bear considering.

The touches came more quickly now, still light and mostly undemanding, but Mathias's whole body felt alight as he tried and failed to anticipate where Pascal would caress him next. The curve of his pec, the inside of his wrist, the line of his jaw, all in quick succession, followed by a long, slow suck of his fingers and then a quick flick of his nipple that made him shout in surprise at the intensity.

"Are you trying to make me come in my pants?"

"The thought occurred," Pascal replied, "but no, not really." He undid Mathias's belt and fly. Mathias lifted his hips so Pascal could strip him. Pascal pushed his pants and underwear down to his knees and stopped.

"No jock tonight?" he teased.

"I was having dinner with your family, not wearing tight jeans to the bar," Mathias retorted. "Real underwear seemed more appropriate."

Pascal laughed. "Somehow I don't think they cared what underwear you had on."

Maybe not, but Mathias would have felt sleazy. He wore the jockstrap under his tight jeans so his ass looked good at the bar. That wasn't the impression he'd wanted to make on Pascal's family. He wanted them to focus on the banker, not on what he was doing now to make ends meet.

"Now," Pascal said, interrupting Mathias's train of thought, "you said something about coming."

Mathias shivered beneath Pascal's intent gaze as he reached for the lube next to the lamp. Mathias tried to spread his thighs, but he could only move so much between his pants around his knees and Pascal straddling his legs. "You're going to have to let me move if you plan on fucking me tonight."

"We'll see," Pascal replied. The promise in his voice made Mathias wonder what else he had planned.

Mathias knew what it felt like to have Pascal's fingers inside him—they'd done that already, more than once—but with every inch of his skin sensitized by Pascal's attentions, the shock of cold lube overlaying the heat of Pascal's fingers caught him off guard, like everything else about the evening had done.

Mathias arched into the caress with a soft, startled noise. He stared at Pascal, lost in the rush of sensation as those long, capable fingers worked his entrance. He braced his feet as best he could, tangled in his slacks as they were, and lifted his hips into the caress. "Please," he begged.

Pascal urged him back down to the mattress, but he pressed inside as he did, which was all Mathias really cared about. He leaned over Mathias again to kiss him. His shirt brushed Mathias's skin, reminding him that Pascal had done no more than take off his jacket at the door. Everything else remained in place. That just wouldn't do. With Pascal's hands both busy, one driving Mathias insane and the other bracing Pascal's weight, Mathias might actually have a chance to get Pascal's shirt open. He made his fingers work despite the sudden jolt from Pascal playing with his prostate and got two buttons undone before Pascal broke the kiss.

"My turn tonight."

Mathias shook his head. "You have to let me take care of you too."

Pascal grazed Mathias's sweet spot with the edge of his nail, wringing a shout from Mathias as his vision whited out. He wanted.... He needed....

Pascal didn't give him a chance to recover enough to finish either of those thoughts. He stimulated the gland over and over until Mathias couldn't think, could barely breathe. He grabbed for Pascal's shoulders to steady himself before he shook apart, a thousand little pieces of shattered bliss with nothing to keep him together.

Pascal leaned in to him. Mathias turned his head for a kiss, but Pascal only rested their foreheads together as he increased the rhythm of his fingers inside Mathias. "Let go."

With a sob, Mathias did, every muscle clenching as wave after wave of pleasure dragged him down into blackness.

When he came back to himself, Pascal was stretched out beside him, one hand resting on Mathias's clean stomach—had he been out of it that long?—and the other propping up his own head.

"Back with me?" Pascal asked.

Mathias nodded, not trusting his voice to work. He felt more than a little loopy.

"Good." He leaned over and kissed Mathias tenderly. The movement brought their bodies into contact, letting Mathias feel the ridge of Pascal's erection beneath his pants. He'd given in and let Pascal take care of him, but he was done being selfish. As good as Pascal had made him feel, Mathias needed to return the favor.

"My turn?" He'd meant the words as a statement, but they came out as more of a question.

"If you want," Pascal replied, "but tonight was for you."

"This is for me," Mathias insisted as he tried to remember how to make his hands work. He fumbled the buttons, but he finally got Pascal's shirt off. He tugged on Pascal's arm to get him to lean over so Mathias could lick one of his nipples while he worked open Pascal's pants. He slid his hand inside, finding hot, slick flesh, and stroked up the hard length to tease the tip. He might not have Pascal's acumen when it came to making every inch of skin an erogenous zone, but he knew what to do with a hard cock when he got his hand on one. He slid the foreskin back to expose the glistening tip and passed his thumb over the slit. Pascal froze and shook beneath the touch, spilling all over Mathias's hand and stomach.

Mathias stroked him through his release automatically, head spinning at the thought that it hadn't taken more than that simple touch to make Pascal lose it. He hadn't expected it to take a lot, but he'd figured it would take more than that.

He cleaned his hand on the edge of the sheet and snuggled closer to Pascal.

"The things you do to me," Pascal murmured against Mathias's ear. "It really should be illegal."

"The things I do?" Mathias parroted. "All I did was start to give you a hand job."

"No, you let me spend all that time making love to you. Then you touched me. That was all I needed."

Mathias didn't see how that computed, but it obviously made sense somewhere in Pascal's head because it hadn't taken much of anything, and Pascal had proven he didn't have a hair trigger usually. Somehow or another, in ways Mathias didn't even pretend to understand, Pascal had gotten as much out of driving Mathias out of his head as Mathias had.

He snuggled closer. "I don't want to go downstairs. My bed's lonely without you."

"Then don't go." Pascal tightened his embrace and kissed the top of Mathias's head. "Just set your alarm early enough that you won't be late because you slept here."

"Really? You don't mind?"

"I was going to ask you to stay. You just brought it up first."

Mathias blinked a couple of times, trying to process his earlier fears about Pascal's feelings to his mother's reaction to them with this new knowledge. If Pascal wanted him to spend the night, he probably wasn't considering whether he should keep the peace with his family.

"It's not that hard a choice, is it?"

Mathias heard an underlying vulnerability beneath the teasing words.

"It's not a hard choice at all. I was just thinking how silly I was earlier to worry that your mother's reaction would cause problems. I'm new at the whole family thing."

"She won't remember it tomorrow, probably," Pascal said. "When she's lucid, she remembers all her other lucid times, but she doesn't remember the times when she wasn't lucid. And when she isn't lucid, it's anyone's guess what she'll remember. The next time she meets you, it will probably be like she's never met you before but wants to because I told her about you on a good day."

Mathias nodded and shifted a little to get more comfortable, which drew his attention to the fact that they were both still partially dressed.

"We should maybe finish getting undressed so we can sleep," Mathias said.

Pascal chuckled and sat up. He stripped off his shirt and skimmed his pants down his legs. "Better?"

Mathias took a moment to ogle Pascal, only partially teasing. He still didn't know how he'd gotten so lucky with his silver fox, but damn, he wasn't going to question it.

"Much better." He stripped quickly as well and sighed in contentment as he rolled back against Pascal.

"Alarm set?"

"On my phone. And it was fully charged before we left today. It will be fine."

"Good." Pascal reached over and clicked off the lamp. He shifted them on the bed until he could spoon behind Mathias. Mathias closed his eyes on the thought that as badly as the day had started, it couldn't have ended any more perfectly.

CHAPTER 21

MATHIAS DID his best to pay attention to the conversation with his colleagues and the representative of the big corporate client they were trying to win over, but they had turned to discussing the latest plays on Broadway, something Mathias had no interest in or knowledge of. He kept one ear open enough that he'd hear if they addressed him directly, but most of his attention strayed across la Colombe d'Or to Pascal as he went about his duties. Mathias had hoped Pascal would be in charge of their table when Louis had told him he would be included at the dinner, but they'd been seated in a different section, with the manager himself dancing attendance on them.

Mathias still didn't know how he'd gotten lucky enough to catch and hold Pascal's attention, but in the two weeks since Thanksgiving, he'd mostly stopped questioning that he had it. He shifted on the chair, still feeling the lingering effects from their lovemaking the night before, when he'd pinned Pascal to the bed and ridden him hard… until Pascal flipped him over and gave him the pounding he'd been begging for. The memory had a predictable effect on his anatomy. He reached for his glass and took a sip of water to cool himself off a bit. He didn't want to have to explain to his boss that he was getting worked up watching his lover across the room.

As good as the sex was—and it got better every time, not that Mathias could explain how—Pascal's attentiveness was even better. They spent every free moment together, and Pascal seemed to be going out of his way to create those moments. They still had Tuesdays off together, but Pascal had joined Mathias for lunch a couple of times when he didn't need to be at the restaurant until later, and he'd invited Mathias to stay any time Mathias was at his place late into the evening, or even if Mathias texted him from the bar and he was still awake. Mathias wasn't one to look a gift horse in the mouth, but he couldn't stop from worrying that it was suddenly too easy. Daniel had treated him that way at first too.

The restaurant door swung open to admit a group of laughing women, one of whom was carrying a basket wrapped in cellophane with a big pink bow and helium-filled balloons attached. Mathias wondered which of them was having a birthday. If nothing else, they might be more interesting than the conversation that continued to drone on around him and safer than watching Pascal. He wasn't likely to end up blushing from watching them instead.

Pascal came out of the kitchen and directly into Mathias's line of sight. He waited, hoping Pascal would look up and smile at him as he'd been doing off and on all night, but Pascal didn't glance his way. He started across the room toward one of his tables when he saw the women with the balloons. In an instant, the professional smile Mathias had been itching to erase all evening changed to the sexy smirk he always gave Mathias right before doing something to drive Mathias out of his mind.

Mathias swallowed around his own reaction to that smirk because it wasn't directed at him. Pascal was heading directly toward the group of women with that look on his face. Mathias's gut churned. It was Daniel all over again. He couldn't make a scene. Not with his boss sitting only a few seats away. He couldn't even excuse himself for a few minutes because he'd already done that not long ago, when watching Pascal had gotten to be too much. He had no choice but to grit his teeth and watch as the women greeted *his* lover with familiar kisses to the cheek and pats on the back. Then the one with the gaudy basket handed it to Pascal amid the raucous laughter of her friends. They made so much noise that it drew the attention of Mathias's colleagues as well.

"I wonder what the occasion is," Louis asked.

Mathias did his best to look uninterested as the others speculated what might motivate that kind of a gift to a waiter in a restaurant. None of the suggestions turned bawdy, much to Mathias's relief. They all had too much riding on the outcome of the dinner to alienate their new client, but that didn't stop the sick feeling growing in Mathias's stomach. He couldn't watch this, whatever *this* was, but he couldn't look away.

Pascal set the basket in the middle of the table and kissed the giver's cheek again. He'd never given Mathias any indication that he was bi, but

Mathias didn't know how else to interpret what he was seeing. He'd met Pascal's sister. Whoever this was, she had a relationship of great familiarity with Pascal, one she was allowed to indulge in public while Mathias had to sit on his hands and pretend he wasn't being eaten alive by jealousy.

He couldn't hear what Pascal said from across the restaurant, but the women all laughed again. He'd waited enough tables to tell when Pascal took their order, but his demeanor never changed back to the cool professionalism he'd demonstrated all evening, even when he left their table and headed back to the bar. Mathias tried not to be too obvious as he followed Pascal's progress. At the bar, the bartender punched Pascal in the shoulder playfully. Pascal laughed and ducked his head a bit, giving every sign of delighted embarrassment at whatever the bartender said. Mathias had reacted the same way when Michel teased him about Pascal at Le Salon. He didn't see how Pascal could be cheating on him with the unknown woman with as much time as they had been spending together, but he couldn't make the pieces fit together any other way.

He tore his gaze away from Pascal and concentrated on his plate. The thought of eating only made his stomach roil worse, but if he didn't, someone would ask what was wrong, if the food wasn't to his liking, something, and he didn't want to make a scene. If he could have figured out a way to leave early, he would have. He'd been looking forward to tonight, to seeing Pascal at work, but now he was wishing he'd found an excuse to bow out of the dinner entirely. Ignorance really was bliss.

PASCAL CARRIED the round of cosmos back to the table where his ladies were waiting. He couldn't believe Martine had made such a spectacle of bringing him her latest book. No, scratch that, he could believe it. The wrapping for the Pascal St. Laurent books had gotten more outlandish with each successive release, but this topped them all. Balloons, for Christ's sake. Then again, it had made him smile, which had always been the point—of the books, of the gifts, of the teasing, of the friendship itself. Sometimes he thought he'd never be able to repay his ladies for everything they'd done for him over the years.

"One round of cosmos for the table," he announced as he passed them around.

"Where's yours?" Camille asked. "We have to have a toast."

Pascal laughed. "Okay, hold on. I'll get Nick to pour me one."

He headed back to the bar, only to be met with Nick's smirk. "You forget something?" he asked, handing Pascal a fifth cosmo. "They always insist on buying one for you when they bring you a new book. I don't know why you thought tonight would be any different."

He hadn't, really, but he also refused to assume on their friendship by having Nick make him one until they invited him. Nick had no such qualms.

He returned to the table with his drink. His ladies picked up their glasses as well.

"To finally getting what you've been waiting for," Martine said, clinking her glass against Pascal's before touching it to the others' glasses as well. Pascal made the rounds as well and sipped the cosmo.

"Does this mean Pascal finally makes a move on Jack?" he asked Martine.

"You'll have to read and find out, won't you?" she said. "But what makes you think I was talking about the book? From what I can tell, you've finally gotten what you've been waiting for too."

Pascal could hardly argue with that. "He's here tonight, you know. You've now thoroughly embarrassed me in front of him."

"Really?" Nicole asked. "Where?"

"Be subtle," he hissed. "I don't know if his employers know he's gay, but even if they do, they probably don't know about me, and I'm not going to be the one to out him at work."

"We know how to be subtle," Hélène replied.

Pascal snorted. "Yeah, about as subtle as a nuclear warhead. He's sitting at the table of businessmen behind me. The youngest one at the table."

"He's cute," Camille said. "You weren't kidding about the young part. He'll keep you young too."

"What, no panther jokes?" Pascal teased.

"Not when he so clearly makes you happy," Nicole replied. "You might think we were discouraging you."

"And that's the last thing we want to do," Martine added.

"That deserves another toast," Hélène said. "To Pascal and his new boyfriend, may they have all the happiness they possibly can."

Pascal clinked glasses with them all again and took another sip of his drink. "Dinner, ladies? Or do you need more time to look at the menu?"

"Give us a little longer, if you don't mind," Martine asked.

Pascal smirked at her. "For you, darling, anything."

They all laughed, as he'd intended. He picked up his drink and left them to make their decisions. He did have other tables that needed his attention, even if Simon had given him fewer than usual when he saw his ladies on the list of reservations.

Pascal glanced toward Mathias's table, but Mathias wasn't looking his way. He also didn't look like he was having a very good time. Hopefully he'd get home in time to cheer him up a bit before they had to call it a night.

MATHIAS DUG his fingernails into the palms of his hands to stop from shouting when Pascal shared a toast with the women. *Don't make a scene. Don't make a scene. Don't make a scene.*

He also couldn't keep watching if he wanted to have any sanity left before the night was over. He'd confront Pascal when he got home from work and find out what was going on, but for now he had to think about something else. More than that, he had a boss and a client to impress, and he couldn't do that sitting here moping because his boyfriend was flirting with someone else. He was better than that, and he was going to prove it. Pascal might not notice, but Mathias's self-esteem demanded it.

He tuned back in to the conversation around him to realize that the topic had moved from Broadway shows to the Canadiens. He might not know anything about theater, but he could talk hockey. Determined not to give Pascal another thought, he joined the debate about who was the better team—the Habs or the Leafs.

MATHIAS MANAGED to keep his promise to himself for the rest of the evening, staying engaged in the conversation as it changed from topic to topic. A couple of times, he thought he caught an approving glance from his boss. Louis certainly smiled proudly at him every time Mathias met his eyes. He hadn't looked across the restaurant at the table of women a single time, no matter how loudly they laughed nor how many times he'd seen Pascal approach their table out of the corner of his eye. He'd let himself get distracted early in the meal, but he wasn't letting it happen again.

His boss paid the bill, and they all rose to leave. Mathias glanced around the restaurant under the guise of gathering his coat and briefcase, but Pascal had his back to him, attention firmly fixed on his table. Pushing down the hurt that Pascal couldn't be bothered to acknowledge his departure, he followed the others out onto the sidewalk. When the restaurant shuttle left to take their client back to his hotel, the others scattered.

"I'll walk with you as far as the métro," Louis said. "You did great tonight. It's not easy, being the new one at a dinner like this, but you stayed in the game. Mr. Belanger was impressed."

"I'm glad," Mathias said. "I was lost for a while there when they started talking theater. Not something I really know much about."

"I bet if you ask Pascal, he'd help you remedy that."

Mathias shrugged, not wanting to think about Pascal at the moment.

"Was he there tonight?" Louis went on, not picking up on Mathias's mood.

"Yes. The silver fox waiting on the table of women with the obnoxious balloons," Mathias said, hoping his bitterness over that fact wasn't too obvious.

"Oh, he *is* a good-looking one," Louis said. "Well done."

Mathias smiled as best he could, though it felt fake. Sure, Pascal was good-looking, but it didn't help his mood to have that pointed out to him. The women had obviously found him much to their liking as well, and not just tonight.

They reached the métro stop and their different directions, saving Mathias from having to reply. "I'll see you in the morning."

"Have a good night," Louis replied with a wiggle of his eyebrows.

Mathias should have laughed. Any other night he would have, but even if Pascal got home soon, Mathias wasn't in any mood for what Louis had suggested. He waved instead and went through the turnstile for his line.

Louis's laughter followed him down the stairs and onto the train.

CHAPTER 22

MATHIAS PACED his apartment, trying to calm down. There had to be a logical explanation for what he'd seen at the restaurant that night. Pascal wouldn't cheat on him, not after making love to him so tenderly the past few weeks. Nobody could be that good an actor. Nobody. Except that he would have said the same thing about Daniel before that all went sour.

He needed to go upstairs and ask Pascal for that explanation instead of making accusations. He could say he'd seen Pascal with his friends, ask who they were, be the loving, curious boyfriend, not the jealous harpy he felt like on the inside. He could be adult about this. He just had to give Pascal time to explain. Once he'd heard the whole story, it would make perfect sense, and he'd be able to laugh at his overreaction. Pascal never had to know what seeing him flirting like that had done to him. It wasn't his usual demeanor with customers, just with those specific ones. Mathias had watched him before they came in, and he hadn't acted that way with anyone else. Pascal would tell him why he acted that way, and everything would be fine.

He just had to stay in control until he could hear Pascal out. He took a deep breath and then another, trying to get enough air into his lungs to calm his pounding heart and escape the tide of emotions that still threatened to drag him under. Pascal wasn't Daniel. He didn't think of Mathias as a piece on the side. He'd taken Mathias home to meet his parents and his sister.

They'd discussed Pascal's schedule. He didn't have to close tonight, so he would be able to leave the restaurant when his last table did. If tonight was anything like the other nights he didn't have to close, he'd be home by eleven thirty. Mathias could wait until eleven forty-five and go upstairs then to talk to him. That would give Pascal a chance to get home even if he was running a little late, maybe to change clothes, but not to be asleep already. Mathias didn't want to wake him up. He just wanted an explanation. If that made him immature, well, he'd have to live with that. After tonight, he needed it. He needed to hear that Pascal hadn't cheated on him the way Daniel would have done. Wouldn't cheat on him the way Daniel had done.

He wouldn't lie in wait in the foyer. He'd stay in his apartment and go up to see Pascal after he got home. The foyer wasn't the right place for the conversation they needed to have, no matter how calm Mathias managed to stay, and if he didn't manage, the foyer definitely wasn't the right place. He just had to be patient until eleven forty-five. Then he could go upstairs and let Pascal tell him it had all been a misunderstanding.

And if it wasn't just a misunderstanding, that was better learned in private too.

He looked over at the clock on the oven. Eleven twenty. Pascal ought to be home any time now. He couldn't see Pascal's window from his apartment or even from his "terrace," so that wouldn't help him. He paced a few more times, trying to bring down the frenetic energy coiling through him, but all the pacing in the world couldn't make the time pass faster.

He'd never make it twenty-five more minutes. He wasn't sure he could make it five. He could go upstairs now and see if Pascal was home. If he was, that would put an end to his waiting, and if he wasn't, walking the stairs would use more energy than pacing his apartment.

That's what he'd do. He'd change out of his suit into something more comfortable and go see if Pascal was home yet. They'd probably run into each other on the stairs, but Mathias wasn't spying, like Daniel had accused him of doing when Mathias finally found out. He was coming to talk to Pascal. He'd just seem a little eager if Pascal wasn't home yet, but there were worse impressions to give.

He went into the bedroom and dug out weekend clothes—not the suits he wore to work or the tight jeans and T-shirts he wore to the bar, but a comfortable pair of track pants and a loose sweatshirt. That struck the right note, didn't it? Relaxed, easy, just coming to check in with his lover before bed. Nothing to be stressed about, no reason to worry. A prelude to a good-night kiss.

If he told himself that enough times, he might even believe it.

He took a deep breath and reminded himself not to make accusations or fly off the handle. Just because Daniel had screwed him over didn't mean Pascal had done the same. He had to give Pascal a chance to explain. Then he could decide how to react. He locked his door behind him and climbed the stairs to Pascal's apartment.

He heard the music playing before he ever knocked at the door. Nothing he recognized, some sort of jazzy number, soulful without being sad. Under any other circumstances, Mathias probably would have liked it, but now it made him suspicious. Pascal didn't usually have music playing. Why did he have it on now?

He knocked because as often as Pascal had invited him to stay over in the past few weeks, he hadn't offered Mathias a key. Mathias hadn't thought anything of it until now. They were lovers, yes, but they weren't living together. Mathias had his own place and liked it that way. Now he wondered why Pascal hadn't even brought it up.

Pascal opened the door almost immediately, still wearing his white shirt and black trousers from the restaurant, although the top three buttons were open now, revealing the white T-shirt Pascal wore beneath it.

"Mathias, I didn't expect to see you tonight," Pascal said, opening the door wider and stepping aside so Mathias could enter. "I was going to text you in the morning in case you were asleep when I got home."

Pascal's easy acceptance of his presence reassured Mathias. Pascal wouldn't let him in so easily if someone else was here. He hadn't brought the woman from the restaurant home with him. Mathias didn't *really* think Pascal would cheat on him that way, but something inside him uncoiled anyway.

Right up until he saw the gift basket in pride of place on the table.

"You couldn't even try to hide it?" Mathias asked, turning on Pascal.

"Hide what?" Pascal asked.

Mathias gestured wordlessly to the basket on the table. "I saw you tonight at the restaurant. What the hell was that? Those women were all over you."

Pascal looked from Mathias to the table and back to Mathias. "My ladies? We were just having a bit of fun."

"I know what a bit of fun looks like," Mathias insisted. "That was more than just a bit of fun."

"You flirt with customers at the bar all the time," Pascal pointed out. "And they're far more likely to act on it than my ladies."

Mathias snorted. "I saw them watching your ass every time you walked away from the table."

Pascal laughed, so loud it startled Mathias. "Oh, Mathias, you really don't get it, do you? Martine and the others have no interest in my ass. It's the fact that I'm tapping yours that fascinates them."

Mathias blinked a couple of times. "What?"

"Open the gift," Pascal said.

Mathias frowned but walked over to the table as Pascal instructed. Conscious of Pascal watching him, he didn't shred the paper like he wanted but opened it carefully to pull out a hardcover book. The title caught his eye. "Wait, is this the new one? It's not due out for another month."

"I told you I know Martine. She brings me a copy as soon as she gets them. I often have them as much as six weeks prerelease, depending on when they can get into the restaurant."

"I don't understand."

Pascal sat down on the couch and patted the space beside him. Mathias perched on the edge of the couch, completely baffled now.

"Martine, Hélène, Camille, and Nicole have been patrons at la Colombe d'Or for as long as I've worked there. They came in regularly even before I waited on them the first time, but since then, they've always asked to sit in my section. We chatted. At first it was casual stuff, the way you do as a waiter to keep your patrons happy, but after a while it went beyond that. And when Robert died and I was so miserable, Martine had an idea to cheer me up." He handed Mathias the book. "She borrowed my name and set out to write a story of a broken man putting himself back together, not miraculously, but piece by painful piece, all the while saving the world one bad guy at a time. There are times I think looking forward to the next book was the only thing that kept me going in those miserably dark days. So yeah, I joke with them. I toast every new release with them. On quiet nights sometimes I even sit down with them and have an appetizer. And yes, they take it upon themselves to embarrass me with each successive release by bringing a bigger, even gaudier presentation than the time before, but it's all in good fun. Tonight, though, I didn't need the balloons and the teasing to cheer me up, because tonight I got to share something with them that I didn't think I'd ever get to say."

Mathias wanted desperately to know what it was, but he was afraid if he asked, Pascal would stop talking.

"Tonight I got to tell them they didn't have to worry about me anymore," Pascal continued without prompting. "I got to point out where you were sitting at the other table and tell them that I was truly, maybe even ridiculously happy because that cute banker at the other table was willing to put up with me, gray temples and all. That toast we drank was to you and me."

Oh fuck.

"I screwed everything up."

"I don't know. Did you?"

"I was so fucking jealous. I couldn't think straight."

"I love my ladies like they were my sisters, but first of all, they're all happily married. More importantly, I'm happy with you. I don't want anyone else."

"I don't know why," Mathias muttered. "When I do stupid shit like this."

Pascal laughed and pulled him into a hug. "You're young. Stupid shit is part of the package, although maybe next time you could try asking me what's going on before you jump to wild conclusions. Martine will be tickled if I tell her she made you jealous, but then she'll smack me for not giving you enough assurances that you don't have anything to worry about."

Did that mean what Mathias hoped it meant?

"Nothing to worry about?" he asked when Pascal didn't say more.

"Not a thing," Pascal said. "I'm totally gone over you. I was just waiting for the right time to tell you. I didn't want to scare you off, but I'm hoping maybe the jealousy means you feel the same way."

All the air rushed out of Mathias's lungs, leaving him feeling like a fish out of water. He blinked a couple of times, trying to make sure this wasn't all a dream.

"Yes," he said finally when Pascal continued to look at him expectantly. "Yes, I feel the same way."

PASCAL SLUMPED against the back of the couch at Mathias's admission. He'd hoped…. God, had he hoped Mathias was starting to care for him too, but he hadn't known how to bring it up without possibly scaring Mathias off. He was fiercely independent, one of the many things Pascal admired about him, but that meant Pascal had been walking on eggshells since he'd realized his own feelings. Asking Mathias to move in was out of the question given how he insisted on paying for half their dates. Even asking him to stay some nights was fraught with worry as to whether he'd gone too far too fast.

Mathias's fit of pique had caught him off guard for a moment, but then he'd realized it was jealousy, and if Mathias was jealous, then maybe, just maybe, that meant he felt something more. That hope had made it easier to stay calm in the face of Mathias's accusations and to explain his friendship with his ladies. Mathias hadn't said the words Pascal longed to hear, but then again, Pascal hadn't said them either, just implied them strongly. And Mathias had said he felt the same way.

"What happens now?" Mathias asked softly.

Pascal sat up and reached for Mathias. Mathias moved into his embrace willingly. "Anything we want," Pascal replied. "We can keep going like we have been. We can move in together, here or somewhere else. We can quit our jobs and run away to Aruba and be beach bums."

Mathias snorted in laughter. "Beach bums?"

"I'll have you know I look quite fetching in swim trunks," Pascal said in mock offense.

"I believe it," Mathias replied, "but I don't see either of us being happy with nothing to keep ourselves busy. We'd end up bored to tears in a matter of weeks."

Pascal smiled and kissed Mathias sweetly. "Okay, so that last part was a joke. I meant the rest of it. What do you want to have happen?"

"I don't want a sugar daddy," Mathias said slowly. "If we move in together, here or somewhere else, I'm going to pay my share of all the expenses."

"That's reasonable," Pascal said. "I never offered to pay for dinner because I thought you couldn't. I'm hardly rich, so it's not like you were trolling me for my money."

"You make more than I do right now," Mathias said.

Pascal shrugged. "Maybe, but at some point that won't be true anymore. Bank executives make nice salaries, but combining expenses and sharing them between us would save us both money, even if we got a bigger place."

"Does that mean you want me to move in with you?" Mathias asked.

"Eventually," Pascal said. "It doesn't have to be this weekend. I don't want you to feel rushed into a commitment you're not ready to make."

"And if I said I wanted to move in tomorrow?"

"I'd get a key made for you on the way to the restaurant in the morning," Pascal replied immediately. He wouldn't press. Mathias had to make that decision for himself in his own time, but now that it was on the table, he wanted it so badly it stole his breath.

Mathias looked around the apartment appraisingly. "Not that I have a lot of stuff, but do you think there's room for both of us here? I don't want us to end up breaking up because we're constantly on top of each other."

"I don't know," Pascal drawled. "I rather like it being on top of you."

Mathias laughed, as Pascal had intended—not that his comment was anything less than the truth. "One of these days maybe I'll be on top."

"Whenever you want," Pascal replied easily. He'd taken charge with Mathias because that seemed to be what he wanted, but he was more than happy to mix things up.

"One of these days," Mathias repeated. That was fine with Pascal too. He certainly had no complaints about reducing Mathias to a shivering mess beneath him, as often as Mathias wanted. "You didn't answer my question."

"I think the only way to find out is to try it," Pascal said. "Robert and I lived in a place even smaller than this for a while, before we could afford somewhere nicer. I moved here not long after he died because I needed a fresh start. If we try it and find we don't have enough space, we can always look for something bigger when the lease is up. Although, there's your lease to think about too."

"I have one more month left on the lease," Mathias said. "I moved in in May and only signed a six-month lease. As much as I wanted to live here, I wasn't sure I could pull it off. Making the smallest time commitment on offer seemed prudent. I could spend more time up here even if I still officially had the apartment for another month. I wouldn't be able to help with rent here until I don't have to pay rent for downstairs, but it would mean we'd see each other more."

"That would be fine, but like I said, it's entirely up to you. I don't want to rush you into something. We can see how it goes over the next month before you give notice. And if you aren't sure, you could go month to month for a while. The landlord will let you do that after the first commitment is over."

Mathias looked at him intently. "You keep saying you don't want to rush me and asking if I'm ready. What about you?"

"I already know what I want, but I'll take whatever you're willing to give me," Pascal said.

"You going to tell me what that is?"

Pascal hesitated. He didn't want to send Mathias running for the hills. "As long as you understand that what I want is only that, not what I expect. Relationships are all about the negotiation."

"I know, but it's a little hard to negotiate when I don't know where you're starting from."

Pascal took a deep breath. This was it. In for a penny, in for a pound. "Okay, then, in an ideal world, you'd move in with me as soon as reasonably possible, we'd pool our resources and see if you can quit working at the bar. I'd look at cutting back my weekend shifts so we'd have that time together, even if I still had to work evenings during the week. You'd take me to meet your parents, and you'd get to know my family better so that you'd know Maman loves you even when she doesn't remember you. Or maybe even so that you'd be such a part of the family that she'd start remembering you the same way she remembers me. At some point we'd get married and grow old together, even if that happens to me well before it happens to you." He took a deep breath, not daring to look at Mathias. "But that's my ideal world. All of it is up for discussion if it's not what you want too."

Mathias squeezed his hand. "We'll have to look at the timeline for some of that, but I don't see why any of it would be off the table. The job at Le Salon is just a way to make ends meet. If we can combine expenses so I don't have to work there, I'll gladly quit. I don't have any real vacation until Christmas, though, and La Tuque is a little too far to go for just a night."

Pascal slumped against the back of the couch, pulling Mathias with him as he went. "As long as I know we're both moving toward the same goal, the timeline is easy."

EPILOGUE

Eighteen months later

PASCAL LOOKED up from serving drinks to Mathias and his friends—he hadn't been able to get the night off to celebrate Mathias's promotion out of the training program and into a full-time position as branch manager for mortgages, but he'd insisted Simon put them in Pascal's section—when his ladies walked in, gift basket in hand.

Mathias winked at Pascal before turning back to Nathalie and Janine, two other trainees in his program, and, of course, Louis. If Pascal were the jealous type, he'd have had something to say about how often Mathias came home from work talking about Louis. He had laughed with Louis's boyfriend about it more than once. "We've lost him now," Mathias said. "He's going to spend the rest of the evening flirting with his ladies, and we'll never get our dinner."

"I would never do that," Pascal said with a mock pout.

"I know better than that," Mathias said. "I've watched you flirt with them before. Go on. Say hello from me too."

Pascal gave Mathias a grateful smile despite the teasing. They'd come a long way since the first time Mathias had been in the restaurant the same night as his ladies. A *long* way. To his surprise, the hostess seated his ladies one table over from Mathias and his friends.

Martine waved at Mathias as they approached.

"I have an idea," Mathias said. "Would you ladies like to join us? That way Pascal doesn't have to bounce back and forth between us."

"We wouldn't want to impose," Nicole said even as Martine's smile widened. Pascal almost said no on principle. He wasn't sure he'd survive Mathias getting friendly with his ladies.

"It's not an imposition," Mathias said. "We're celebrating. It's not a business dinner. Although it looks like you're celebrating too."

"Just bringing Pascal his usual gift," Martine replied. "It comes out in two months, but this one is extra special, so I made sure to get an advance copy just for him."

Pascal took the package she handed him, balloons and all.

"Why is this one extra special?" he asked.

"Open it and see."

Pascal didn't usually open the books they brought him until he was home and could enjoy them in private, but Martine was looking at him expectantly, not to mention Mathias.

"Let me pull the tables together, if you're going to do this, and then I'll open it."

"Are you sure you don't mind?" Martine asked Mathias.

"I'm sure."

Pascal set the gift basket in front of Mathias with a stern, "Don't touch," and gestured for another waiter to help him move the tables together. Once everyone was situated, he took the package back and unwrapped it carefully.

At the top of the cover, even above the title, the words "The Long-Awaited Conclusion" jumped off the page.

"What's this?" he asked Martine.

She smiled up at him from her seat. "When I started the series, it was to cheer you up and give you hope where you didn't see any. Last I heard, there's a wedding in the works. Seems like you got your happy ending, so I thought it was time to give my fictional Pascal his as well."

"I'll drink to that," Mathias said, raising his glass.

"Hold that thought," Pascal replied. "I haven't brought drinks for everyone. I'm sure Nick has your drinks ready. Let me get them, and then we can have a toast."

Nick had a tray of five cosmos ready to go when Pascal approached. He carried it back to the table, served his ladies, and took his own drink.

Martine lifted her glass. "To happy endings."

Pascal met Mathias's gaze as everyone clinked glasses and smiled at the pure, unadulterated joy that matched what he felt perfectly. Yes, he'd drink to that.

When ARIEL TACHNA was twelve years old, she discovered two things: the French language and romance novels. Those two loves have defined her ever since. By the time she finished high school, she'd written four novels, none of which anyone would want to read now, featuring a young woman who was—you guessed it—bilingual. That girl was everything Ariel wanted to be at age twelve and wasn't.

She now lives on the outskirts of Houston with her husband (who also speaks French), her kids (who understand French even when they're too lazy to speak it back), and their two dogs (who steadfastly refuse to answer any French commands).

Visit Ariel:

Website: www.arieltachna.com
Facebook: www.facebook.com/ArielTachna
E-mail: arieltachna@gmail.com

ARIEL TACHNA

AT YOUR
Service

When Anthony Mercer walked into Au cœur du terroir, he was looking for good food and a pleasant evening spent with a friend. He never expected to meet—and sleep with—Paul Delescluse, a waiter at the restaurant. After spending a magical week together in Paris, Anthony must return to his life in North Carolina, while Paul remains in France.

Despite the distance and the lack of promises between them—Paul wants sex, not a relationship—Paul and Anthony forge a solid friendship. Then Anthony's job takes him back to Paris, this time to stay. Paul is thrilled to have him back, but Anthony has a harder choice: be another of Paul's conquests or fight for the relationship he knows they could have, if only Paul would believe it.

www.dreamspinnerpress.com

CHECKMATE

Nicki Bennett
and
Ariel Tachna

All for Love: Book One

When sword-for-hire Teodoro Ciéza de Vivar accepts a commission to "rescue" Lord Christian Blackwood from unsuitable influences, he has no idea he's landed himself in the middle of a plot to assassinate King Philip IV of Spain and blame the English ambassador for the deed. Nor does he expect the spoiled child he's sent to retrieve to be a handsome, engaging young man.

As Teodoro and Christian face down enemies at every turn, they fall more and more in love, an emotion they can't safely indulge with the threat of the Inquisition looming over them. It will take all their combined guile and influence to outmaneuver the powerful men who would see them separated… or even killed.

www.dreamspinnerpress.com

ALL FOR ONE

Nicki Bennett and Ariel Tachna

All for Love: Book Two

Aristide, Léandre, and Perrin pledge only three loyalties in life: their king, their captain, and their passion for each other. So when the musketeers discover a plan to accuse M. de Tréville of treason, the initial impulse to kill the messenger, Benoît, is tempered by their need to unmask the plotter. But their first two suspects, the English ambassador and Cardinal Richelieu, prove to be innocent, forcing the musketeers to delve deeper into the inner machinations of the French court.

Meanwhile, Aristide finds himself falling in love with the ill-fated messenger, a blacksmith without a home who rouses all of his protective, possessive instincts. Benoît, however, has no interest in any man. Torn between desire and duty, Aristide must find a way to protect the king and clear his captain's name—all while heeding the demands of his heart.

www.dreamspinnerpress.com

STRONGHOLD

Nicki Bennett
and
Ariel Tachna

All for Love: Book Three

"Are you surprised that strength is drawn to strength?"
For the last six years, the gypsy healer Raúl has lived a life he
never dreamed possible. Gerrard Hawkins has stood at his side, his love
a source of silent strength like nothing Raúl has ever known.

When a letter from Gerrard's estranged father forces them in
separate directions—Gerrard back to England to make peace with his
family and Raúl to Saintes-Maries-de-la-Mer for his annual pilgrimage—
Raúl expects to suffer for their parting, but he holds on to their plans to
meet again in France when Gerrard has satisfied his father's demands.

Gerrard left England never expecting to return, especially after he
pledged his life and love to Raúl. Yet he cannot dismiss his father's offer
of peace without some acknowledgment. When he arrives in England to
find tragedy, his sense of duty toward his family's tenants wars with his
promises to Raúl.

As tensions mount and illness spreads in France, Raúl stands as a
bastion of hope, but his strength is not limitless. Gerrard is the rock he
leans on, and without that strength, Gerrard's arrival in France may come
too late.

www.dreamspinnerpress.com

DREAMSPUN DESIRES

Ariel Tachna

UNSTABLE
STUD

*Lexington
Lovers*

Horses were his passion, until he laid eyes on his boss.

Lexington Lovers

Horses were his passion, until he laid eyes on his boss.

Eighteen months ago, tragedy struck Bywater Farm when a riding accident killed Clay Hunter's lover and traumatized his prize horse, King of Hearts. Clay and King lingered in limbo, surviving but not really living, until a breath of fresh air in the form of Luke Davis, a new groom in the stud barn, revives them both.

When a fall from King's back sends Luke to the emergency room, Clay watches the shaky foundation of their budding relationship tumble down. Can Clay really love a jockey again, or will his fear of losing another man he loves keep them apart for good?

www.dreamspinnerpress.com

DREAMSPUN
DESIRES

A MATCHLESS
MAN

Ariel Tachna

Lexington
Lovers

*None of the matches
caught his eye as much
as the matchmaker himself.*

Lexington Lovers

None of the matches caught his eye as much as the matchmaker himself.

Growing up poorer than poor didn't leave Navashen Bhattathiri many options for life outside of school. All of his concentration was on keeping his scholarships. Sixteen years later, he's fulfilled his dream and become a doctor. Now he's returning home to Lexington and is ready to prove himself to the world. In doing so, he reconnects with Brent Carpenter—high school classmate, real estate agent, all-around great guy… and closet matchmaker.

Brent makes it his mission to help Navashen develop a social life and meet available, interesting men. Unfortunately Navashen's schedule is unpredictable, and few of those available, interesting men value his dedication like Brent does. Brent's unfailing friendship and support convince Navashen he's the one, but can he capture Brent's heart when the matchmaker is focused on finding Navashen another man?

www.dreamspinnerpress.com

FOR **MORE** OF THE **BEST GAY ROMANCE**

DREAMSPINNER
PRESS
dreamspinnerpress.com